The Young Man and the Sea

Rodman Philbrick

THE
YOUNG
MAN
and
THE
SEA

SCHOLASTIC INC.

New York Toronto London Auckland Sydney
Mexico City New Delhi Hong Kong Buenos Aires

The author wants to thank Paul Brown, of Kittery, Maine, for his insights into the fine art of trapping lobsters. Also, some of the amazing physical abilities of the bluefin tuna were gleaned from Douglas Whynot's book *Giant Bluefin*.

This book was originally published by the Blue Sky Press in 2004.

ISBN 0-439-36830-8

12 11 10 9 8 7 6 5 4 3 2 1   6 7 8 9/0

Printed in the U.S.A.   40

First Scholastic paperback printing, March 2005

FOR MY BROTHER JONATHAN,
WHO KNOWS WHERE THE BIG FISH LIVE,
AND FOR MY FEARLESS NIECES,
MOLLY AND ANNIE PHILBRICK

Contents

1. LOBSTER BOY   9

2. SWAMPERS   14

3. BY THE BARREL RAISED   20

4. ROTTEN TO THE KEEL   27

5. ATTACK OF THE VAMPIRE MUD
   WORMS   35

6. THE FINEST KIND   42

7. THE RINGING OF THE HAMMER   48

8. WHAT THE GREASE MONKEY SAID   53

9. MONEY BY THE POUND   59

10. LOBSTER IN THE PARLOR   66

11. TRAP WARS   73

12. RICH BOY IN THE DARK OF NIGHT   80

13. WHEN YOU WAKE UP   88

14. BY HOOK AND BY CROOK   98

15. WHERE THE BIG FISH LIVE   107

16. THE BLUSHING BANDIT   113

17. THREE RULES FOR SKIFF BEAMAN   119

18. WHAT HAPPENED TO THE STARS   125

19. IF MIST MADE THE WORLD   133

20. TAKE MY BREATH AWAY   140

21. WHEN THE WHOOSH COMES BY   149

22. KEG RIDER   158

23. A NANTUCKET SLEIGH RIDE   166

24. THE ANGEL IN THE MIST   174

25. THE TAIL ON THE DOOR   189

1

Lobster Boy

BEFORE I tell you about the biggest fish in the sea and how it tried to kill me and then ended up saving my life, first you got to know about the leaky boat, 'cause it all began right there. The great repair and the trap wars and the angel in the mist, none of it would have happened without the leaky boat.

It starts the last day of school. I'm on my way home, coasting down Spotter Hill on my crummy old bike. The birds are chittering and stuff, and I'm riding no hands with the wind on my face. A day like that you can feel summer in the air, and the smell of cut grass, and the sting of salt from the harbor. Then our little house comes into view, and right away I see that what I been afraid of these last few months has finally happened.

Our boat the *Mary Rose* has sunk at the dock.

It breaks my heart to see her so pitiful, with just the top of her cabin showing, and a shine of oil spreading like blood on the water. A sunk boat is a pitiful thing. It's enough to make a person cry, but I ain't cried since the day my mom died. No matter what that rotten rich kid Tyler Croft says, it ain't true.

I been bailing *Rose* for months, getting up before dawn to pump out the bilge and keep her floating. Just in case my dad decides to get his lazy duff off the TV couch and go fishing. That's where he lives ever since the funeral, lying like a sack of nothing on the TV couch. Most times he don't even put the TV on, he just sucks on his beer and stares at the cobwebs on the ceiling.

It ain't like he's a real drunk. He don't beat me or curse me or nothin'. He just lies there feeling sorry for himself and it don't matter what I do or say. One day I swore him out for ten straight minutes, about how he was a good-for-nothing and a worthless boozer, and how he might as well be dead as lying on the TV couch, and what would Mom think if she could see him. But even that don't get him going. He just sighs and says, "Skiffy, I'm awful sorry about everything," and then hides his head under the pillow.

I can't even be sure if he's talking to me or to himself, 'cause we got the same name. Samuel "Skiff" Beaman. Down the town wharf they used to call my dad Big Skiff and me Little Skiff, to tell us apart, but my dad don't go down the wharf no more. He don't do nothin' at all. Not even when I come running in the house to tell him *Rose* has sunk.

"Dad!" I go. "She gone under!"

He rolls to one side and puts a bleary eye on me. His beard is all matted because he ain't combed it in months, and it makes him look old and scruffy. "School's out, huh? How'd it get to be that late?"

"The boat sunk! What'll we do?"

"Do?" He puts his hand over his eyes and sighs again. "Oh, I suppose we could raise her up, but she'd just sink again. Best leave her be."

"You can't leave a boat sunk at the dock. It ain't right!"

But my dad turns his face to the back of the couch and won't hear me, so I run outside and skid down the steps to our rickety old dock, but there ain't nothing I can do. Once a boat has gone under, you can't bail it no more. There's nothin' to do but wait until the tide goes out and then somehow winch it onto the cradle before it sinks again. Then maybe I can find the leak and plug it.

There used to be a winch in the trap shack, and that's where I'm heading when Tyler Croft comes by on his thousand-dollar mountain bike and thinks he sees me cryin', which he don't.

"Hey Skiffy!" he goes, popping a wheelie and showing off. "Heard that old wreck of yours finally went under. Good riddance! Ugly thing stunk up the whole creek. That wasn't a boat — it was an outhouse!"

"Shut up!"

"Ooh, Skiffy's cryin'!"

"Am not!" I said, looking around for something to throw at him, a rotten apple for his rotten head.

"Skiffy's cryin' and I ain't lyin'! Little Skiff Beaman lives in a shack, he pees in a bucket and craps out back! Hey lobster boy! Your momma's dead, your daddy's drunk! Go back to the swamp, you dirty punk!"

I been hearing variations on that stupid song since Tyler Croft was old enough to talk, so it don't mean nothin'. All it does is make me want to womp his head with a hard green apple because that would make him cry.

There's nothing close to hand but an old chunk of wood. I heave it and miss. Tyler laughs and then screams away on his bike.

"I'm tellin' the whole wide world!" he shouts back over his shoulder. "Little Skiff Beaman cried like a baby!"

He will, too. Not that it really matters. When your whole life is sunk, it don't matter what nobody says about you, they can't make it worse.

Still, I wish I had that hard green apple.

2

Swampers

I GOT to admit, what Tyler Croft says is partly true.
Our little house used to be a shack, until my mom
married my dad and made him fix it up. I wasn't
there, of course, but I seen the pictures. We got running water now, and indoor plumbing, but my dad
never seen no reason to tear down the old outhouse
with the half-moon carved in the door. Says it reminds
him of the way things used to be, and how cold it was
on winter nights when you had to put on your hat and
boots just to do your business in the outdoor toilet.

When I was real little I remember my mom used to
always be at him to take down that ratty old out-

house, but then she got used to it and planted flowers around it and painted it up and stuff, and didn't mind too much when folks came round to see what it looked like, because it's the last outhouse in all of Spinney Cove. Kind of historical, you might say.

My dad's family, the Beamans, they was swampers. That's local talk for white trash, I guess. In the old days, swampers was folk who lived in shacks near the salt marsh or on the creek, and got by digging clams and trapping crabs and lobster and selling salt hay to the farmers. Come fall they'd shoot ducks and geese and salt 'em down and sell 'em by the barrel to restaurants in Boston. The point is, they lived off what they got from the marsh and the creek. This is way back before my dad was born, but they still called him a swamper on account he was a Beaman, and Beamans had always been swampers, simple as that.

My mom, now, she weren't no swamper, not even close. Her people was Spinneys that settled here and got the town named after them, or maybe they named it for themselves, same difference. There are rich Spinneys and poor Spinneys and regular Spinneys, but there ain't no swamp Spinneys, and my mom's family never let my dad forget it, believe you me. Mom never liked that, and stood up for my dad. She always said we all came from the same place, if you go back far enough, and what did it really matter what names they put on the headstones?

The name on her headstone is Mary Roselyn Spinney Beaman, so you might say she got to have it both ways.

One thing with swampers, though, they're good with boats. It's in our blood, I guess. When I was nine, my dad nailed up a little skiff for me out of plywood, and put an old five-horse Evinrude motor on the back, and give it to me for my birthday, which was really cool.

I'm twelve now, but the skiff still fits me pretty good, and don't leak a drop. "A tight boat is a good boat," my dad used to say, but now he don't care if the *Mary Rose* sunk, so it's up to me to raise her.

Only thing, I don't really have a clue how to go about it — I never raised a sunk boat before. So I get in my skiff and row around above where she went under. I can see her down there sitting on the mud, but it still don't figure, what to do next. Finally I get sick of looking and decide I'll row up the creek to Mr. Woodwell's place and see if he has any ideas on the subject.

Lucky for me, he does.

Mr. Woodwell is about a million years old now, and mostly retired, but once upon a time about half the working boats in Spinney Cove come out of his shed. He built the *Mary Rose* before I was born, and I seen the picture of him standing by the bow when she got launched for the first time. Even in the picture he looks quiet, and it's only got worse since then. Folks say he's so shy with words that weeks go by between one sentence and the next. That may be, but he always says hello to me. "'lo, Samuel," he'll say. "Come alongside and tell me what the fish are doing." And I'll put in to his dock and tell him the smelt are running or the mackerel are in, or if the stripers are feeding. He don't fish — never has — but he likes to know.

The day the *Mary Rose* went under he's planting a bed of flowers by his back porch, the one that faces the creek, and don't see me till I holler. It's too far for him to holler back, so he waves his hat instead, and I put my skiff in to his dock and walk up the grassy slope to the porch.

"'lo, Mr. Woodwell," I say.

"'lo, Samuel," he says, patting dirt around his flowers. "What are the fish doing today?"

"I don't know," I say. "*Rose* has sunk and I can't raise her."

It takes him awhile to get up from the flower bed and wipe the dirt from his hands. "Come up the porch," he says, and I do.

He fetches lemonade, and that takes awhile, too. Everything takes awhile with Mr. Woodwell, 'cause he moves so slow, but I don't mind. You never tasted lemonade so good as what he makes in his steel pitcher, from real lemons and white sugar stirred in.

"There you are," he says, handing me a glass. "I've been worried about that boat," he says, easing himself down into his rocker. "You've been pumping the bilge out regular?"

"I bailed her just before I went to school, and when I got home she was down."

"What did your father say?"

"Nothin' much."

"So it's up to you, is it?"

"I guess."

Mr. Woodwell sips his lemonade and stares out at the creek. "I won't say anything against your father," he says.

"I don't care about him," I say. "I care about the *Mary Rose*."

He gives me a hard look, to see if I mean it, which I do. "Okay then," he says. "I'm too old to be raising sunk boats. I can't hardly lift a hammer, let alone a thirty-six-foot hull."

"But you can tell me how."

"Yes," he says. "That I can do."

3

By the Barrel Raised

O LD Mr. Woodwell, he give me a list of things I need to raise the *Mary Rose*. Fifty feet of rope, a ten-foot plank, and some big steel barrels, what sometimes they call drums. I guess he knew we'd have such things close to hand — every dock on the creek has drums and rope and an old plank or two. Anyhow, first thing I do is fish the rope out of the bait shack. Then I drag a plank out of the woodpile and set it on the dock. The plank has a little green moss along the edge, but it's still plenty strong. There's half a dozen empty steel drums behind the bait shack, and I roll out the four have the least rust. All of 'em got rainwater sloshing around inside, so I tip each one up and empty it out, then fix the cap down tight to make it watertight, or nearly so.

"Four drums will lift two thousand pounds, approximate. That should be just enough to shift the keel," Mr. Woodwell told me. "You put that rig in place and then let the tide do the work."

His idea is tie two barrels to each end of the plank, then run a rope from one end of the plank down under the back end of the *Mary Rose* and up to the other two barrels.

When the tide comes in, the big steel barrels will float up and lift the boat.

"Sounds awful easy," I told him.

"A thing doesn't have to be difficult if you give it some thought and apply a little elementary physics."

To look at him, you wouldn't think Mr. Woodwell was so smart, but he is. My dad used to say a good boatbuilder was partway an artist and partway a scientist, and it was the science part of Mr. Woodwell that was going to help me raise our boat.

Not that my dad cares. Never even sticks his head out the door to see what all the fuss is, with me banging barrels around and talking loud to myself, like I'll go, "Guess I'm on my own out here!" and, "Sure could use a hand with this heavy plank!" and, "Anybody know how to tie a good knot?" and so on.

Finally I give up trying to rouse him and concentrate on rigging the barrels like Mr. Woodwell told me. What sounded dead easy takes me all the rest of the afternoon and partway into the evening. That's okay because the tide won't turn until about nine tonight.

I get it all rigged with an hour or so to spare, so I figure to cook supper for me and Dad while I'm waiting for the tide. He don't care about food much these days, but you got to eat.

"Don't trouble yourself," he says from the couch. There's a show on the TV he's pretending to watch.

"No trouble at all," I go. "Easy to cook for two as for one. You'll need your strength if you're gonna help me with the boat."

He sighs kind of heavy and goes, "Nothing to be done, even if we raised it. She'll just sink again."

"Maybe not."

"Salt water kills an engine dead, once it gets inside. Boat's no good without an engine."

"Here. Eat your spaghetti."

I'm pretty good with store-bought tomato sauce. The way you do it is add fried sausage and onions and cover the whole mess with grated cheese. Spaghetti's fine, I give you that. But by rights we should be eating fresh cod and lobster, only you need a boat to catch 'em. Which I figure to do myself, if Dad can't be bothered.

See, I got it all figured out. Raise the boat, fix the leak, fix the engine, then go fishing. Supposedly I ain't tall enough yet to steer *Rose* by myself, but if I stand on a milk crate I can see good enough. It'll be fun, fishing on my own, and when Dad hears about me working the traps, it'll shame him into helping.

That's my plan. But when my dad gets a beer from the Frigidaire and goes back to the TV couch, all he says is, "Be careful. I couldn't stand it if you drowned yourself."

I go, "You could give me a hand," but he don't say nothing back.

Outside, it's real still, like it gets when the sun has just gone down and the tide is about to change. Like the world is holding its breath and you want to hold yours, too, to make it last. I climb out on the plank and tighten up the ropes some and then there's nothing to do but wait. Hoping that old Mr. Woodwell got it right, and the tide will lift the boat. I'll save worrying about the ruined engine for later.

All the barrels have to do is raise the boat clear of the bottom, then I can pull the bow onto shore. I got that rigged, too, a one-ton come-along winch where all you got to do is crank the handle. That was my idea, and Mr. Woodwell approved.

I'm thinking about all these things at once: the tide coming in, the barrels floating over the sunk boat, what happened to the boat when it went underwater and how much of the gear got ruined, my dad on the couch. My dad on the couch and the summer ahead of me like a big blue train I'm chasing.

I'm thinking so hard, I don't hear Captain Keelson rowing down the creek.

"Skiff Beaman!" he says, loud enough to jog me. "What's up, Little Skiff?"

Captain Keelson is leaning on his oars. Even in the dark I can see the worry on his face. He ain't near as old as Mr. Woodwell, but he's pretty old. He says the rowing keeps him young, but if you ask me, it don't show much.

"Boat went under," I tell him.

He nods. "Yup, I can see that. You rig those steel drums by yourself?"

"Mr. Woodwell told me how."

"Ah yup. What happens when she lifts?"

I tell him about the come-along winch. He thinks about it and nods again. "Should work," he says, talking in his slow way. "Where's your paw?"

"Just nipped inside. He'll be right out."

"That so? Well, you give him my regards."

Then he glides away, dipping his long oars into the water so smooth and soft, it makes me wish I could be rowing, too, out on the creek in the dark, rowing away from everything.

Thinking about rowing on the dark water makes me tired and I lie back on the dock for just a little while, with the current humming around the pilings. Moving water sounds sleepy, like a tired person going "shush," and before you know it I'm flat-out fast asleep.

In the dream I'm adrift on the current in a leaky boat in the dark of night and can't find my oars and can't see the shore and can't do nothing to save myself. I want to shout out for help but my voice don't work and it don't matter anyhow because there's no one can hear me.

What finally wakes me is the barrels nudging against the dock, *bonk-bonk*, and the top of the *Mary Rose* white as the moon, raised up from the bottom, come back to life, just waiting on me to fix her.

4

Rotten to the Keel

MY dad never does come out to see the boat. When I wake him up on the TV couch and tell him the *Mary Rose* is high and dry, he looks at me like he don't understand.

"How'd you manage that?" he asks.

When I explain about the barrel rig, he shakes his head. "All on your lonesome?" he says, like I bragged on going to the moon and back and he didn't quite believe me. "A twelve-year-old boy, and small for his age?"

"I ain't that small! Plenty boys my age are smaller'n me. Besides, a thing don't have to be difficult if you give it some thought and apply a little elementary physics."

I knew that one would stump him, if he didn't guess I'd borrowed it from Mr. Woodwell. But as nice as he was being, acting all impressed, it still wasn't enough to shift him off the TV couch and see it with his own eyes.

I'm bone-tired from cranking on that winch but too excited to go to bed yet, so I go out on the dock and stand there under all the stars and admire the boat. What with the dark and the deep shadows, you can't tell how hurt she is, or know the engine is probably ruined. At night she don't look much worse than the last time she was hauled out for painting, more than a year ago.

They say a thing that's broke can always be fixed, if you work at it. And that's what I intend to do, no matter what.

When morning comes, I'm up with the sun, busting around the kitchen like an itch you can't scratch. That's what my mom used to say when I got an idea in my head and wouldn't be shut of it. This morning my idea is pancakes first and then fix the boat. I'm a demon for pancakes. That's another thing my mom used to say. I'm in mind of her because of the boat, I guess. But Dad don't want to hear nothing about Mom; he says it only gets him down and what's the use and better not to think about it.

So far he's been doing a pretty good job of not thinking about much of anything, but he don't say no to a plate of pancakes.

"These Aunt Jemima from the box?" he asks.

"No, she come over and helped me mix 'em up from scratch," I say. "What's a matter, they don't taste good enough for you?"

"No, no. They're perfect, Skiff. Delicious. I didn't mean — they remind me . . . oh, never mind."

Pancakes ain't supposed to make you look like you want to cry. Me, I'm feeling fine and dandy; I won't let no blubbery looks ruin what I got in mind for the morning, which is fix the boat, have lunch, then go fishing.

The boat got a different idea. When I crouch and look under, down at the bottom by the keel, I can see where one whole plank has come loose. I poke at her with my jackknife and the wood is soft and crumbly. Rotten. I can't figure what to do about it, so I climb in the boat and pull up the floorboards and look at it from that side.

One thing I know, you ain't supposed to see daylight when you look at the bottom of a boat. This is bad, real bad. I'm worried maybe the whole of her is rotten and can't be fixed. That she'll never float again. That all my plans for the summer are just plain stupid, and Tyler Croft is right about me being a swampy good-for-nothing.

Or maybe I ate too many pancakes and the syrup has gone to my head. Like Mom used to say, looking at the thing won't fix it. And since I ain't got the first clue where to start, I get in my skiff and row up to Mr. Woodwell's place again.

When I get there he's out in the shed where he used to build his boats. It's a big, spacey kind of building with windows high up, and daylight coming down in beams, and the clean smell of wood shavings in the air.

He's standing by the tool bench but not working on nothing. Just smoking on his corncob pipe and looking kind of wistful. Thinking about the empty shed, I guess, and all the boats he built there.

" 'lo, Samuel," he says. "Did she rise?"

I tell him everything worked just like he said it would, and the *Mary Rose* is high and dry, but now I'm stumped. I tell him about the plank that sprung loose near the keel, and how I'm pretty sure it's gone bad.

Mr. Woodwell puffs on his pipe for a bit. "Your dad could repair that, no trouble at all. He knows about such things."

"He's not in the mood for fixing stuff."

"But you're willing?"

I nod. "Only I don't know how."

Those cool gray eyes of his kind of soak me up as he thinks about it. When he speaks it comes out deliberate and careful, like always.

"You're willing to learn, I can see that. Mmm," he goes, puffing on the cob. "I'll have to survey the damage. Yup, that's the first thing. Can you get me down there in your skiff, do you think? To the scene of the crime?"

The old man takes a long time lowering himself

from the dock to the skiff, but I know better than to rush him. Once he's settled, I row out into the creek and let the current take us.

Mr. Woodwell trails a hand in the water and smiles with his eyes, staring off at the tall pine trees along the shore. "Been some time since I've been out on the creek," he says. "Thank you."

"I ain't done nothing. You're the one doing the favor."

That makes him chuckle deep in his throat. "You always say it straight out, don't you? Much like your father. Did you know he worked for me when he was your age and a bit older?"

"Sure," I say. "He still brags on it."

"Does he now? He was a quick study, Big Skiff was, and a hard worker. By which I mean he worked hard to get it right, whatever he did. Could have been a fine boatbuilder if he'd had a mind to. But the sea drew him. Wanted that open sky around him. Finest kind of fisherman, your father. Best man with a harpoon in Spinney Cove, no doubt about it."

"I guess."

"It's still there. Give him time."

"Yes, sir, I will."

But really I'm thinking, what can you do with a man who blubbers when you make him pancakes?

I give Mr. Woodwell a hand getting from my skiff to our dock and it's amazing how light he is, for a grown-up. Like his bones are hollow or something.

"There now," he says, straightening up. "I'll take just a minute. If I move too fast, my head forgets where it is."

"Yes, sir."

"Do you know how old I am, Samuel?"

"No, sir."

"I'll be ninety-four in August. I was an old man when your father came to work for me, and that was many years ago."

"Yes, sir."

"My eyes aren't so good, but I can still see a thing by touching."

"Yes, sir."

"I'm telling you this because it will take me some time and I'm asking you to be patient. Boys are not patient creatures, as a rule."

I swear to him I'll be patient, but waiting for the old

man does try me. Watching paint dry is a speed sport compared to watching Mr. Woodwell inspect *Rose*. He touches every part of her with his skinny bone-looking old hands, from the bow all the way along the keel to the stern. He has to bend over to get under the boat, and I can see it hurts him, but there's a look in his eye that says don't say nothing, and I don't.

It's getting on to noon when the old man finally works himself out from under the boat. "You may help me stand," he says, holding out his hand.

I help him up. He takes a deep breath and finds his balance.

"Could be worse," he says.

"The boat," I say, "or you?"

That gets him laughing until his eyes are wet. "Oh, you are a spark, Samuel." He takes a breath that whistles inside his nose. "Now, the boat. Garboard planks are rotten on both sides of the keel, but the keel itself is sound enough. There's nothing that can't be repaired. No reason the *Mary Rose* can't be made as good as new."

That makes me so happy, I run up to the house to tell my dad, even if he don't care right now.

5

Attack of the Vampire Mud Worms

I'm wrong about Dad, sort of. Turns out he's pleased about the boat, or anyhow about Mr. Woodwell helping me fix her.

"Good old Amos," my dad says, sitting up on his couch. "I most forgot he was still alive! Amos Woodwell! Yup, he give me a hand when I really needed it, way back when."

"He said you could have been a real fine boatbuilder, if you wanted."

"Amos said that?" my dad goes, acting pleased. "I don't know. There was a time I followed him around like a little puppy dog. Things were pretty bad at home, if I remember correctly, and I moved into Amos Woodwell's boat shed for the summer and partways into the fall. He taught me a few things. Not just boats."

"Mr. Woodwell says there's nothing wrong with *Rose* that can't be fixed."

He nods and rubs his eyes. "Amos'd know. She was one of the last boats came out of his shed."

I ain't seen my dad acting this interested in anything for a long while, but it don't last. When I start telling him what we got to do, pulling off the bad planks and stuff, his eyes get that look that means he's not listening and pretty soon he's staring at the TV again and sighing. The sighing part really gets my goat.

I suppose a really good son wouldn't try to shame his father, but I can't help it, the words just come out mean. "Hey, Dad? I'm off to get the toolbox. You recall the toolbox? Man needs tools to work. Screwdrivers and hammers and stuff. Plenty of tools there, you want to help," and so on.

Might as well talk to the TV, for all the good it does.

———

The *Mary Rose* is waiting for me with her bad side turned up, like a dog holding up a hurt paw. Mr. Woodwell says the only thing I need right now is a screwdriver and a pry bar, but I bring along a hammer, too, just in case I want to hit something.

"Hello, Rose," I say, sliding under the bottom and wiggling my way down to where the keel sits in the mud. It's drippy under there because the planks are still weeping and you got to be careful of barnacles. Barnacles are sharp as razors if you hit 'em just right.

"Mr. Woodwell says I got to pry off these two planks, Rose. I hope you don't mind."

Sounds pretty crazy, a boy talking to a boat, but I always talked to that boat, ever since I was little. My mom used to say don't worry unless the boat talks back to him. It ain't happened yet, and I don't expect it ever will. But that don't stop me trying.

"Weren't your fault you sank," I tell her. "That was us, not taking care of you. Hold on now, this won't hurt a bit," I say, trying to work the pry bar along the plank that came loose. Being careful, 'cause Mr. Woodwell says we need the whole thing in as near as one piece as I can manage, so we can trace it out and cut another just like it. But the rotten plank is stubborn, and I have to leave off the pry bar and dig out the screws that hold it to the ribs.

Takes me most of the day to back out the screws. And I have to keep apologizing to the boat for swearing every time I scrape my knuckles on a barnacle.

"Ouch! You miserable . . . stinking . . . scum-sucking . . . stupid barnacle!"

I'm still trying to work the first plank loose when something bites me in the back. I sit up quick and bump my head against the plank, and that don't improve my language. Then it bites me again and suddenly a bunch of things are down inside my underwear, wriggling around and nipping at me.

That gets me crawling out from under the boat as fast as I can. It ain't until I'm standing up that I figure out what's going on. Mud worms! I been lying on one place for so long, they finally found me. I'm mad enough to spit, and scared, too, because they won't stop biting.

The only thing I can think to do is strip off my pants and jump in the water. That works. When I hit the cold water and give my underwear a shake, the worms let go. But it ain't over, not quite. Soon as I wade back to shore and pick up my pants, this monkey starts hooting at me. Monkey by the name of Tyler Croft.

"Hooey! Lobster boy! That where you take a bath, that dirty old creek?!"

Just my luck. Tyler and a couple of his rich-kid buds from up the cove. Joey Gleeson and Parker Beal. Parker ain't no bigger than me, but hanging with Tyler makes him think he's tough, I guess. All three of them showing off on their fancy mountain bikes.

"Hey Skiffy!" goes Parker Beal. "Is that mud on your underwear or did you poop in your pants?"

"Come on down here and find out," I tell him.

No chance of that. Might ruin his hundred-dollar shoes. After a while they get sick of calling me names and ride away laughing.

Maybe I should feel bad, getting made fun of like that, only it seems so stupid, I can't take it serious.

Bloodsucking mud worms, now *that's* serious.

No point telling my dad about the worms, he'd only say a swamper boy should know better than to lie down in the mud. Anyhow, by the time I get cleaned up he's already had a bunch of beers and don't want to talk.

Like I said before, some kids when their fathers drink, they bust up the house or hit their mom or worse. Not my dad. He just lies on the couch and don't say nothing. Only way I can tell is the smell of beer and the way he breathes sort of heavy.

"'lo, Dad," I go, "mind if I watch?"

He makes a grunt that means "go ahead," and I flop down in the ratty old chair by the ratty old couch and stare at the screen. Actually it's a show I like, about cops and lawyers solving crimes and stuff, where everything gets settled in the end. Wouldn't that be great, if everything really fixed itself that easy? Like if because I raised the boat my dad would quit drinking and turn over a new leaf or something.

It don't work that way in the real world. Still, even with the beer and all, it's sort of cool, the two of us watching the same show and probably thinking the same things about it.

In the end he's asleep before the show gets over. I

already know what happens, so I turn off the TV and go, "Sleep tight and don't let the bedbugs bite."

When I'm halfway up the stairs, he calls out, sort of sleepy, "Your mother used to say that."

"She still does," I say, because it's true inside my head.

He don't say nothing to that.

6

The Finest Kind

ONE of the best things about Mr. Woodwell's boat shed is the clean smell of wood shavings and varnish. It sort of clears my head to take a deep breath. Even the smoke from his little corncob pipe smells good, the way it blends in.

When I drag the bad planks into the shed, he's sitting on a stool at his workbench, sharpening his chisels on an oil stone.

"'lo, Samuel," he says without looking up. "Lay those down on the sawhorses, if you please, next to the cedar planks."

I lay 'em down and rub my hands on my pants. "Took a lot longer than I figured."

Mr. Woodwell nods as he wraps his chisels up in soft cloth. "That's the way it is with boats."

I reach in my left pocket and pull out an envelope. "I only got twenty-eight dollars for the new wood right now," I tell him. "So can we go up to that and then stop?"

The old man smiles. "I figured to charge you exactly what I paid for it," he says, "which was nothing."

"Somebody gave it to you?"

"My father did, many years ago. He left me a woodlot full of prime white cedar. That's how I first got started in the business of building boats. Had to do something with all that cedar, didn't I?"

"I guess."

"So you can put the money away. You're going to need that and a lot more to repair the engine, when it comes to that."

We go over to the sawhorses and he shows me how to clamp the old plank onto the new wood and trace around it with a pencil. When I'm done tracing he has me take the clamps off and carry the new plank to the band-saw table.

"We'll have to be very careful," he says. "Keep your hands well away from the blade."

"You want me to cut it?"

"My eyes are weak, Samuel. I can't see the line. I'll guide you through it. First rule: Never rush a cut. Second rule: Let the blade do the cutting. Don't force it. Third rule, especially for beginners: Don't cut too close to the line."

We position the new plank on the cutting table. The old man presses a button, and the band-saw blade starts running. "Ease it forward," he says putting one hand on the plank, near mine. He can tell I'm scared to make a mistake and ruin the plank. "Can you steer a small boat into the current?" he asks.

"Sure. That's how I got here."

"Think of this plank as a boat. You're steering the plank so the blade stays on that side of the line."

It makes sense. At first I'm sort of wobbly and worried the blade will get ahead of me, but then I realize the blade don't move, the plank does, and nothing won't happen until I make it happen, and from then on we're okay.

After I get the plank cut out, Mr. Woodwell has me set it in his bench vise and he takes up a block plane. "This part I can still manage," he says.

What he does is feel along the edge for the pencil mark, and shave off the wood real smooth until it's just touching the line. "How does it look?" he asks. "If the line disappears, you tell me."

I go, "It's perfect, Mr. Woodwell," and that makes him smile and nod to himself, like he wasn't sure he could still do it until he started.

After we get the new plank shaped, we take a break so Mr. Woodwell can puff on his cob pipe for a while and I can drink lemonade and have a plate of cookies to keep up my strength. I'm munching a cookie and gandering around the shed when I notice this big old harpoon up on the shed wall, sort of hiding in the shadows. The kind of skinny, wicked long harpoon used for giant tuna, like my dad used to catch before he switched to TV and beer.

"That was your father's," Mr. Woodwell says, when he sees me looking. "Shaped it himself, that year he worked with me. Last thing he ever made in this shop. Left it here as a memento."

"What's a memento?"

"A token of friendship. Something to remember a person by."

Mr. Woodwell looks like he's got more to say, but he holds back. I guess he knows I ain't in a mood to talk about my dad right now, or what a great harpooner he used to be, or how many big fish he caught when times were good.

When the old man finishes his pipe he goes back to his bench and takes out a different plane. He explains that the new plank needs a beveled edge so it will fit up tight against the keel.

"This is the tricky part," he says, showing me what he's doing. "Fortunately I know that particular keel pretty well, and remember where it curves."

"You want me to do it?"

"Rather you watch and make sure I don't make a mistake."

The old man is pulling my leg, of course. I bet he ain't made a mistake in a long time. You can tell the way he holds the plane and skates it over the edge. The way he makes the shavings flutter down into thin little pieces of wood that look like curly wings.

"Smell that?" he asks. "Fresh-cut cedar, like they'll put in a chest or closet to keep the moths away. This particular plank has been seasoning here in the shed for near on twenty years, but it still cuts fresh. Nothing like it."

It takes us the rest of the day to get the new planks ready. When they're done, Mr. Woodwell suggests we stand back and admire our work.

"Not bad," he says, nodding with satisfaction, "not bad at all, for a young boy and an old geezer with bad eyes. I think we're a pretty good team, Samuel, don't you?"

"Yes, sir," I say. "Finest kind."

7

The Ringing
of the Hammer

PUTTING on the new planks takes two whole days. I learned my lesson with the mud worms, so I drug out an old piece of plywood and lay on that. Then I clamped the plank to the ribs like the old man told me, and drilled holes for the new screws. Then I put the screws in, all one hundred and ten of them, and that took forever. Then I had to put in the plugs that covered the screws, and that took forever, too.

Got to know the bottom of that boat real good. Every dent and seam, every place it had ever been repaired.

"Won't be long now," I keep telling her. "'nother day or two you'll be floating on your own. Maybe the engine ain't ruined and you'll take me fishing and make us some money, hey Rose? You were always good at finding fish."

One time Captain Keelson rows over and checks out the job. He used to be a tugboat captain, and tugboats are made of steel, but he knows a thing or two about wooden boats and gives me a thumbs-up on what I done so far.

"Heard from Amos Woodwell on the telephone," he says. "Asked me to set the cotton when you're ready, with your permission."

That makes me laugh, a fine and proper gentleman like Captain Keelson asking my permission to help. Setting the cotton has got me worried, because the old man says if it ain't done right, the boat will still leak, even with new planks.

The day we're ready, *Rose* and me, they both come by, Captain Keelson and Mr. Woodwell, together in the captain's red Ford pickup truck. The old man has brought a canvas tool bag that holds caulking irons and a big wooden mallet, and a coil of fluffy white cotton. He hands it all over to Captain Keelson. "Make her ring true, Alex," he says.

The way it works is, you shove cotton into the seam between the plank and the keel with a caulking iron, which is like a dull chisel with a wide blade. Then you womp on the chisel with the wooden mallet and drive the cotton home. If you do it right, the caulking iron makes a ringing noise as the mallet strikes. Then later, when the wood swells up in the water, it will press the cotton tight and keep the plank from leaking.

Mr. Woodwell says they been doing it pretty much like this since the first wooden boat was built, and not to worry, it'll work just fine.

My job is to move the caulking iron along the seam while Captain Keelson hits it *womp!* with his big wooden mallet. "I will try my best not to miss," he promises.

He don't miss, not once in two hours, and I'm grateful for that. But still, my hands hurt from gripping that iron. By the end it feels like the ringing of the mallet comes from deep inside my bones.

After the cotton is set, Captain Keelson crawls out

from under the boat and dusts himself off. He goes, "I leave the rest to you," and he and Mr. Woodwell sit on the dock and watch me fill the seams with tubes of caulking compound. They holler stuff like, "This is the life, watching a boy do a man's job! Stick to it or the caulking will stick to you!" and so on, but I don't mind. It's not like Tyler Croft ragging on me or nothing. Old guys like them only tease you if they like you.

When I finally crawl out, Captain Keelson shakes his head and goes, "Young man, I hope you got as much caulking on the hull as you got on yourself," but I'm too tired to joke back.

Tired as I am, I can't wait for tomorrow. That's when we'll see if the planks hold and keep the water out. That's when we'll know if the *Mary Rose* is ready to go fishing.

I decide from now on if my dad don't bother asking about the boat, then I won't bother telling. I'm sick of pushing stuff on him that he don't want pushed. All it does is put me in a mood, and believe me, that ain't a pretty sight. When I'm in a mood I get all sulky and just want to be miserable. It's like when I'm in a mood, being miserable is the only thing that makes me happy. Weird but true.

So, no moods, thank you. Just make Dad his supper and see he eats some of it. Take out the empty beer cans and hide 'em in the shed so the guys who pick up the trash won't have nothing to talk about. Go to bed early and read my stash of comic books, the ones I found in the shed about The Flash and Green Lantern and Batman before he was a movie. Except I've read 'em so many times, I'm not really seeing the page, I'm seeing the *Mary Rose* and worrying she'll leak as bad as she did before, and sink again. And I'll keep trying to fix her and she'll keep sinking, and that's when I know I'm asleep and dreaming, but there's nothing I can do to make myself wake up until the alarm clock finally goes off.

Brinnnnng, brinnnnng.

Bring me some luck, please. I sure could use it.

8

What the Grease Monkey Said

WHEN the morning tide comes in, I'm ready. Got the winch rigged at the deep end of the dock, to pull the *Mary Rose* free of the shore. Got lines fixed to tie her alongside the dock so she don't drift away. Got my fingers crossed, and my toes crossed, too, hoping she won't leak too bad.

It's one of them soft and misty mornings on the creek. Happens in the summer when the water starts to warm up. Ain't thick enough to be a proper fog, mind you, just a thin, wispy mist that leaves everything kind of blurred. You can't quite tell where the shore lets off and the water begins, and the tall pines look like they're melting into the sky.

There's almost always good fishing when the mist comes on the creek. Fish like to feed in the soft light. Normal times, a day like this, I'd be out in my skiff looking for striper swirls. Instead, I'm waiting with my stomach all clenched up like somebody punched me. Wanting to get it over with, the not being sure.

Can't hurry the tide, though. Tide has a mind of its own. Eventually it does cooperate. When the water's lapping around the high marks on the pilings, I give the winch a couple of cranks until the line goes tight. Then I wait a few minutes and do it again. And again.

That's how the boat comes free, a few inches at a time. About as much fun as watching ice melt — until all of a sudden the winch line goes slack and the *Mary Rose* is floating free.

It seems too easy somehow, and that makes me worried what I'll find. But when I hop aboard and crawl into the bilge to look, the boat is dry inside. No leaks to speak of. I run my hands over the new planks and find a few beads of moisture at the seams, but from what Mr. Woodwell told me, it don't amount to nothing.

"Thank you, Rose," I tell her, "for not giving up."

I'm thinking maybe I should jump up and yell "hurrah!" or something when I hear footsteps coming along the dock.

My dad is standing there, pale as milk.

"I'll be darned," he says, rubbing his eyes. "You did it."

But he don't sound happy. And he looks like he's seen a ghost.

Mike Haley, the diesel mechanic, comes by in the afternoon like he promised when I found his number in the book.

"Big Skiff around?" is the first thing he says.

"He's got the flu," I tell him.

"The flu, huh?" Mike looks up at the house like he don't quite believe me, but then he lets it go. "Heard the *Mary Rose* sunk at the dock. Figured your dad would call me."

"He don't much like the phone."

Mike gives me a funny look. "Is that right?"

"I can pay you to look at the engine." I show him the envelope. Same envelope I offered to Mr. Woodwell.

Mike shakes his head. "No charge for a consultation. Hope you aren't expecting good news on an engine that's been submerged in salt water."

"But you can fix it."

"Depends. Let me have a look."

He climbs into the cockpit with his wrench box. The engine cover is stuck where it swelled up. That makes him sigh and shake his head, like the whole idea of a sunk boat turns his stomach. He goes at the hatch with a pry bar. The hinges sound like a cat with a stepped-on tail, but he gets it open.

"Here goes nothing," Mike says. Talking to himself, not to me. He climbs down beside the engine. I can tell he don't like me staring at him, so I go sit on the end of the dock and wait for him to finish.

It don't take long.

"Skiffy? That what they call you?" He sits down beside me, clears his throat, and spits into the creek. "Wish I had better news, son. I'm just an old grease monkey, but I've been climbing around boat engines for long enough to know the score."

"So can you fix it?"

He looks at me kind of sorrowful. "You mean like add some oil, turn the key, and off she goes?"

"Whatever," I say, embarrassed that he read my mind.

"That would be a miracle, kid, and in my experience, miracles don't happen to boat engines."

"So it can't be fixed."

"Hang on now. Hear me out. It's not as simple as can it be fixed or not. The exhaust manifolds were about rusted through even before she sank. They'd have to be replaced. Starter is shot, and diesel starters are pricey." Mike's talking faster and faster, like he's getting rid of words he don't like. "All new wiring," he goes, counting on his fingers. "New batteries. It may need new pistons — can't tell until I pull the head. New main bearings, that's a certainty. So the answer is, yes, I can fix it, but we're talking a major rebuild, okay?"

"How much?" I ask, thinking of my pitiful little envelope.

Mike sighs like he's the one been sunk. "Even with the fisherman discount, you're looking at a five-thousand-dollar job. Minimum. Could go higher, I start tearing her down and find something else."

I don't know what to say. Five thousand dollars is a mighty big chunk of money. If my dad was fishing, he might get lucky and make that much pretty quick. Once when the tuna were running he made enough in a month to buy an almost-brand-new pickup truck. But he can't fish without a boat. So it might as well be five million as five thousand.

"Tell you what," Mike says. "Have your father call me. I'll tell him myself."

Probably he says some other stuff before he leaves, but I'm not listening. I'm scheming how to find a way to make five thousand dollars before the summer is over, and that about fills up my whole brain.

9

Money by the Pound

"So what did Mike say?" my dad asks.

I tell him the short and sweet of it.

"Five grand, huh? I figured a lot more."

"Do we have the money?" I ask.

Dad shrugs himself around on the couch, so he's staring at a different part of the ceiling. "You know we don't," he says.

"Then it don't make no difference, does it?"

He shades his eyes and looks at me. "Don't be mad at me, Skiffy. I couldn't stand it if my own son was mad at me."

That makes me feel pretty rotten, because it's true.

But I know it ain't fair to be mad at my dad because we're poor, so I go, "Ready for some lunch? Today is grilled cheese day."

By the time the sandwiches are ready I'm over feeling low. Because I got a plan to get the money and solve all our problems.

All along I been concentrating on *Rose*, getting her fixed. I been thinking so hard on that, I forgot she ain't the only boat in the world. There's the skiff my dad built me for my ninth birthday. I been up and down the creek in it a million times, and all over the harbor, too. It's a good little boat, and the outboard runs most of the time. No reason the skiff can't be put to work earning money.

After lunch I get out the calculator.

Okay, here goes. Figure my skiff is big enough to hold me and three lobster traps. Three at a time. There are two hundred perfectly good traps stacked on the dock right now, all licensed and tagged, not doing nothing since my dad quit fishing. If I bring 'em out three at a time I can be fishing all two hundred traps in a couple of weeks.

This time of year they're paying two bucks a pound for lobster at the co-op. So figure two thousand five hundred lobsters equals a rebuilt engine for the *Mary Rose*. Sounds like a lot, but that means each trap has only got to catch about thirteen lobster and we're home free.

Thirteen lobster. That's all. That's the magic fix-the-engine number. Thirteen for each trap and I got all summer to catch 'em. That's like two lobster a week in each trap! This is going to be so easy, I can't think what I was so worried about.

Best thing of all, I can start right away.

There's really no point letting Dad know, but I'm so excited, I tell him anyhow. He looks at me waving a sheet of paper with all my calculations on it and he closes his eyes and sighs.

"It ain't that easy," he says. "You're forgetting what it costs for bait and lost traps and gas for the outboard. And sometime the lobster don't cooperate, you know that."

"The point is, I'll be making money."

"Boy your age should be playing with his friends."

Like I said, no point telling him. All he looks at is

the bad side. Like why bother if things are going to go wrong? He's been like that since Mom got sick and stays that way no matter what I say or do.

It ain't an easy thing, but I got to forget about Dad on the TV couch and concentrate on my own stuff. Maybe he'll come around and maybe he won't, but in the meantime there's lobster out there just waiting to crawl into my traps.

Money by the pound. Easy pickings.

First day after lunch I work like a demon dragging traps to my skiff. Lobster trap is an awkward thing to handle because the weight is all in the bottom. That's to make it sink, of course. But it means I need to be careful how I load the traps into the skiff, so I don't tip the boat over.

Once I get the first three traps into the skiff, I fire up the outboard motor and take us down the creek and into the harbor and up to the wharf at Murphy's Bait & Fuel. I leave five dollars in the jar for a bucket of bait and try to skedaddle before anybody thinks to ask what I'm up to. They're pretty busy salting down a new load of herring, but Devlin Murphy, the boss and owner, he gives me the eye and comes over before I can get away.

I can tell he wants to talk and I'd rather not.

"Bucket of bait? If your old man is back fishing, he's going to want it by the barrel."

I go, "Yes, sir. See you later," and try to scoot out the door.

"Not so fast!" Devlin says, laughing through his beard. He's this huge guy with a big chest and belly and legs that look like tree stumps. He hooks a finger in my shirt and slows me up. "What are you up to, Skiffy? This bait for your dad or what? Heard you fixed the *Mary Rose,* is that it? He finally getting back into it, is he?"

Devlin Murphy is a fiend for gossip. Always wants to know everything that's happening on the creek and round the harbor. My mom used to say he was better than a radio station for having all the local news, and he'll keep at you until you tell him every little thing, even if you don't mean to.

I finally have to tell him the bait is for me.

"Oh," he says, "you going to fish a few traps this summer? Good for you, son."

He follows me out to the wharf and spots the skiff tied up at the end. "Hey, I remember when Big Skiff built that! Lovely lines. You think you can haul up a trap all by yourself?" He laughs and squeezes the muscle on my arm, and that gets me riled.

"For your information, I'll be fishing all two hundred traps," I go, bragging on my own idea. "If you don't think I can pull 'em, just watch me."

That shuts him up, but only for a second. All of a sudden he's looking serious. "What about the *Mary Rose*? I heard you and Amos Woodwell fixed her up."

I shrug. "Bad engine. We're saving up to have it rebuilt."

He scratches at his thick red beard, wrinkles his fat nose, and studies me. "Uh, yuh. That makes sense. Let me think on this. Two hundred traps from a ten-foot skiff. Mmm. That's a whole lot of traps to be hand pulling, young Skiffy. Your dad worked that many with a full-size boat and a hydraulic puller."

"I got the skiff," I tell him, "so that's what I'm using."

He rubs the top of my head, which I hate more than anything. "Tell you what," he says. "We'll set up an account for you, like I did with your father. Give you the fisherman's discount. You can charge the bait and gas you need, and we'll settle up at the end of the summer. That okay with you?"

"Sure it is. Thanks, Mr. Murphy."

"My customers call me Dev. Now you go on and catch a ton of lobster, son. And tell your father Dev Murphy says hello."

He stands there at the end of the wharf, big as his own bait shack, and watches until I'm out of sight.

10

Lobster in the Parlor

THINGS go real good the first two weeks. I'm up with the sun every morning, raring to go. Have my toast and cereal and then run for the dock. Check to make sure *Rose* ain't leaking — nope, dry as a bone — and then drag traps out to the end of the dock and lower 'em into my skiff.

If you do it right you don't have to lift much. Trap itself ain't that heavy, but it's got bricks in the bottom to make it sink. Anyhow, I'll load on, fire up the outboard, go down creek to the harbor, fetch a bucket of bait from Dev Murphy, then off again to wherever I'm setting traps.

Setting traps, that's where the science comes into it. Everybody says so. You got to put your trap where the lobster lives. Lobster crawls along the bottom eating what it can find. So you got to think what the bottom might be like even if you can't see it. Watch where the current whirls, and how the shore comes down. Try to picture it down there. Mostly it's a feeling you get, that this is a good place to set a trap.

'Course there's about a hundred other guys setting traps, too, and you got to take that into account. Set too close to one of theirs, they don't like it. What they'll do is tie a hitch in the line to your buoy, as a signal to back off. That's if they're being nice. Push it far enough, buoys get cut. Then you got a trap on the bottom and no way to find it. Which don't do nobody no good.

Anyhow, by the end of the first week I get near a hundred traps in the water, all baited and waiting for visitors. The old saying is, first the kitchen, then the parlor. See, a trap is divided into two "rooms." First room the lobster crawls into is called the "kitchen." Kitchen has the bait bag and the lobster wants to get at it. But when he tries to leave the kitchen, only place he can go is the "parlor," and there's no getting out of the parlor. Lobster is stuck in there until you pull the trap.

Only thing, pulling the traps out of the water turns out to be a whole lot harder than putting them in.

I wait four days and then go back to the first string of traps. Can't wait to see what it caught. Picturing it chock-full of two-pound lobsters. But when I grab hold of the buoy and start pulling in line, it don't budge. Trap feels like it's been nailed to the bottom.

I cleat down the line, rub my hands together, and try again. This time it shifts a little, but then the rope slips through my hands and the trap clunks back on the bottom.

How can a thing that's made of wood and sunk in the water feel so heavy?

Finally I figure a way to pull the rope up and keep it cinched around a cleat so it don't slip back, and that's how the first trap comes up, a few feet at a time. By the time it comes over the side, slick and dripping, my arms are shaking from the effort.

But that don't matter because there's stuff in the trap. Lobsters, lots of 'em, and a bunch of crabs.

Trouble is, all but one of the lobsters is too small to keep. They're real strict about that. It makes me sick, having to throw back the shorts, but you got to do it.

Still, I do get one keeper.

One down and two thousand four hundred and ninety-nine to go.

"Wake up, Skiffy."

I jump up. Has the alarm gone off? But I'm in the living room not my bedroom and it ain't morning it's night, or getting there. Must have dropped off accidental.

"Figured to let you sleep," says my dad. "You want, I'll fix us some supper."

"Got twelve keepers and a bucket of crab," I tell him.

"So you said. That's good."

I can't recall the last time my dad fixed supper. It's only hot dogs in the fry pan, but still, that's something. Nothing wrong with dogs and beans. Except my hands are so tired and achy from hauling traps, I can barely hang on to the fork.

"Had me a string of traps when I was your age."

"That so?" I go, watching him crack open a beer.

"Thirty traps, that's all it was. Kept me awful busy, though. Thought my arms was going to fall off the first few days. Then I got used to it."

"I'm already used to it."

"I'm just saying," he says. "Two hundred traps. It's possible you bit off more than you can chew."

I go, "That's your opinion."

He sucks on the beer. "Dev Murphy give you credit?"

"Yup."

"Thought he might."

I'm figuring this is the start of a long yammer. Him telling me what to do and so forth, and stuff about what it was like when he was my age. Like dads and sons are supposed to do. But he picks up his beer and goes back to the TV couch. End of conversation.

Anyhow, the dogs were tasty.

Food makes me sleepy again, and I just about crawl up the stairs. Must have, because that's where I wake up the next morning, in my own bed.

Stupid alarm going *brinnnnng, brinnnnng,*

brinnnng. Bring me some lobster, bring me some money, bring, bring, bring.

What I really feel like is rolling over and hiding my head under the pillow, but there's bait to fetch and traps to pull, so I get up and dress and eat and do it all over again.

And again.

And again.

After a while it ain't as hard. Traps don't seem quite so heavy. Bait bucket is lighter. I can work all day and stay awake for a whole hour after supper. End of two weeks all two hundred traps are fishing and I'm pulling twenty-five a day by hand. Averaging a pound and a half per trap, keeper size, and more crab than I know what to do with. Can't get nothing for small crab, nobody wants it, too hard to pick the meat out, but I don't care. I'm a lobster boy, and all I care about is them crawly bugs with the big claws. Money in the bank.

My brain is humming like a cash register, totaling it up, making change. Take out for gas and bait, I'm still ahead by nine hundred dollars, and next week looks to be better, everybody says so.

Like I say, things are going real good. So naturally that's when the crud hits the fan.

Miserable rotten crud by the name of Tyler Croft.

11

Trap Wars

ONE day I'm leaving Murphy's, loaded up with bait and a couple of traps that need new heads. Heads are the little nets the lobsters crawl through to get into the trap. Anyhow, I'm feeling real good about things and minding my own business, and that's when I notice *Fin Chaser* tied up to the town wharf.

Beautiful boat. Finest kind of tuna boat. Forty-foot hull with a high tower on top for spotting fish, and a bow pulpit near as long as the boat. The idea is, the long pulpit puts the harpooner right over the fish so he can strike down at them before they feel the boat.

I never been out on *Fin Chaser,* but I know all

about it because my dad used to be the best harpooner on the crew. Come August he'd lay up the *Mary Rose* and mate on *Fin Chaser* for a month or so. Fished the boat from Provincetown to Bar Harbor, chasing the big tuna. Sometimes he made more money in that one month than all year lobstering.

One summer my dad harpooned eighteen tuna, twice as many as the next best man in Spinney Cove. That's the year he got his new Ford pickup, and Mom got her new kitchen. He and the *Fin Chaser* owner were really tight until Mom got sick and Dad quit working. Then the *Fin Chaser* guy said something to my dad about him drinking too much, or maybe they argued about money, I'm not really sure, and my dad said something back, and they ain't spoke since.

The problem is, the guy who owns *Fin Chaser* and used to be my dad's best friend? He's also Tyler Croft's father. And there's Tyler on his father's boat, loading the long harpoons aboard and acting wicked cool while his dad, Jack Croft, dumps buckets of ice in the ice hold, getting the boat ready.

Last thing in the world I want is Tyler to notice me, but he does. Gives me a big sneery smile, points at my little skiff, holds his nose. I ain't close enough to hear, but his father says something sharp, something that wipes the sneer clean off Tyler's face, and then Jack Croft himself looks at me. Short, strong-looking guy with a long-billed cap, and his eyes all squinty from looking for tuna. Studies me and don't say nothing, just gives me a little nod like they do. Then he's talking to Tyler and pointing at me, like he's saying something about me, and Tyler, he sneaks me a look that says, just you wait, lobster boy, just you wait.

Don't have to wait long.

Next day I'm out by Little Sister Rock, just outside the cove. Got a dozen traps set in close to the rock where the lobsters like to hide. It's one of those perfect summer mornings. Water like rippled glass, with just a few soft clouds in the sky, and everything sparkling. The way the sun comes off the water, it's hard to see at first. But I get in as close to the rock as I dare, with the sea slurping over the top and the seaweed floating like a woman's hair, and I pull up the first trap.

Empty. No lobsters, no crabs, no bait left in the kitchen. Nothing.

Most traps have at least a crab or two, but it happens.

I put the bait bag in the kitchen, drop it back down. Then I grab the next buoy, pull on the line until I feel the trap lift off the bottom. Wrapping line around a cleat as I go, so I don't lose it. Get the next trap up to the side, grab the end, haul it over the side.

Empty. Same thing as the first. No lobster, no crab. And this time I see where the bait bag has been cut loose. By something sharp enough to cut the head net.

Could be a lobster claw, but where's the lobster? Did they get smart all of a sudden and figure a way to back out of the trap? Don't seem likely.

I got a sick feeling in my stomach that it's something else.

Pull the third trap. Empty. Same as the other two.

Pull the fourth.

Pull the fifth.

Pull the sixth.

Empty, empty, empty.

Take a break, my arms aching. Sun drilling a hole in my head. Then haul another six traps, inch by inch. Foot by foot. All empty. Bait bags cut.

Hits me like a bad clam for breakfast. Somebody is stealing my lobster. Worse, they're cutting out the bait bags so the traps won't attract any more lobsters to replace the ones they stole.

Whoever did this wants me to know.

Only one name comes to mind, would do a thing like that. Tyler Croft. Must have snuck out here and emptied out my traps, letting me know he's better than me. 'Course he knows I can't prove he done it. Could have been anybody. But it wasn't. I know that like I know the smell of a rotting fish.

That makes my whole face hot, but it gets worse.

On the way back in I stop to check on another spot, on the inside bend of the channel where the bottom is rocky.

There's not a buoy of mine in sight.

Ten more traps clean gone. Either stolen or the buoys cut, which amounts to the same thing,

Now it feels like my head is going to explode. The only thing I can think of is, open up the throttle and head over to the town wharf, looking for *Fin Chaser*. But the big boat ain't there. Must be out chasing tuna.

I'm so miserable mad, it hurts, but there ain't

nobody to hit or cuss, so all I can do is go home and mope around, thinking of things I'd like to do to Tyler Croft.

Tie his stupid mountain bike around his neck and throw it in the harbor, and that's just for starters.

Later on I'm banging cupboards and stuff, feeling sorry for myself, when Dad wakes up on the couch. "What's wrong, Skiffy?"

"Nothin'!"

"Must be something."

"What do you care! Go on back to sleep! Watch your TV shows! Drink your beer!" I say that and a whole lot more, mean as a snake to my own father.

Worst thing is, he don't say nothing back.

No way can I sleep. Not with Tyler out there stealing lobster and cutting buoys. I got to do something, but I don't know what. Find a way to stop him before he puts me out of business.

Just hating the miserable little twerp ain't enough. I been racking brains and nothing comes to mind. Call him names? He don't care. Throw rocks at his head?

He'd throw 'em back, and plenty would pitch in to help. Call his father? I know Tyler, he'd just lie to his dad and keep on with what he's doing. Report him to the Fish & Game? I ain't got proof. Tell my dad? Don't make me laugh. If he wouldn't get off the couch when the boat sank, he ain't gonna move his butt over a few traps.

What it comes down to is this: It's up to me.

That's why, when midnight comes, I sneak out of the house, get in my skiff, untie the lines, and drift down the creek, quiet as the night.

Watch out, rich boy. Lobster boy is coming to get you.

12

Rich Boy in the Dark of Night

THE thing about drifting the creek at night is how it makes you feel invisible. Like you can watch the darkness of the world go by but nothing can see you. You can see the tall pines standing like an army of zombies along the shore, with stars for eyes and the wind moving their ragged arms, but they can't find you. Nothing can.

It's like being asleep but watching yourself inside the dream, drifting on the creek. Letting the tide pull you around each bend. Letting the current carry you along but keeping you always safe, always moving.

Until you wake up and remember that what you've

always been afraid of has already come true. Like what happened to Mom and the *Mary Rose* sinking. Makes you never want to wake up, but in the end you got no choice, that's the way it works in this world. You got to wake up, or disappear.

And I ain't about to disappear. Not without a fight.

I can't know what buoys he'll cut next. All I can do is try and guard what's mine. Figure a sneak like Tyler will take the easy way, and hit the traps closest to home. The Croft house is way out on the east end of Spinney Cove, with all the other big houses. Places where they got electronic gates and garages big enough for six cars, and more rooms than people to live in them. Rich-people houses. Houses so important, they got names, like Windswept and Beach Rose and Seaview. Rich guys like Tyler's dad, they don't fish for money, they fish for the fun of it, and because it gives them an excuse to own a big expensive boat and wear a long-billed fisherman's cap.

Nothing wrong with that — you can bet I'd have a wicked big boat if I were rich, and a new hat, too! — but it gets my goat when rich people steal from me. And that's what cutting traps is, plain and simple:

stealing. Sticks in my craw like a rusty hook, knowing how little it means to a rich creep like Tyler Croft, that he can ruin my life anytime he feels like it.

There's no moon in the sky, but the stars make enough light to see by, just barely. Enough so I can find my way, weaving through the boats moored in the harbor. Shadows of boats is more like it. Looming things that move with the current, swinging all together like a flock of ducks set down on a pond, beaks to the wind.

Sound of my outboard echoes off the hulls. So loud, it seems the whole world must know where I am. But they don't. It's just another sound in the night, a small boat going by, no big deal.

Just beyond the harbor, striped bass are feeding on baitfish in the shallows, making a noise my dad used to call "fish grenades." Kind of a hard, wet smack. Big fish eating little fish. You can tell by the way they hit sometimes, that the little fish gets away.

I like it when that happens.

I'm easing in along the shore, about a hundred yards from the Crofts' big floating dock, when a boat pulls away from the dock. I quick shut off my motor and lie down in my little skiff as it goes by. When I peep over the side, there he is: Tyler Croft taking off in *Boy Toy,* his own personal Boston Whaler. Brand-new four-stroke outboard runs so quiet, all you can hear is the slap of water on the hull. Perfect for sneaking around at night. Doesn't have his running lights on, so I know he's up to no good.

Trouble is, he's going so fast, he's almost out of sight before I can get my little five-horse motor started. All I can do is follow along in his wake. But that's enough to get a pretty good idea of where he's going. The curve inside the jetty where I set a dozen traps. If he's really there, cutting my buoys, I'll have to sneak up on him. Otherwise he'll just take off and I'll never catch him.

Once I get to where the jetty starts, I turn off the motor and get out the oars. Row up close to the jetty and then follow it along. Jetty is like this big arm made of rocks that pokes out into the harbor and protects it from waves whenever there's a storm. Right now it's hiding me in its shadow as I row along. Being careful as I dip the oars. Splash might give me away.

As I row I'm looking over my shoulder. Wishing I

could see in the dark like a cat or something. I do see something out there, but what is it? Could be just a boat anchored on its mooring, farther away than I think. Distance is hard to judge at night, on the water, with only the light of stars to guide you. But then something moves on the boat and I know.

A person standing up. Then leaning over the side of the boat. Then standing up again. Can't quite make it out, but it's got to be Tyler, grabbing my buoys in the water and cutting the line, then moving along to the next buoy. Must be it's too much work to actually haul up the trap and steal the lobster. Easier just to cut the buoy.

I keep rowing until I get opposite the dark boat. Then I take hold of the starter cord and pull, praying my outboard motor will fire up on the first go.

It does.

I got no plan in mind except how mad I am. So I twist the throttle and head for the dark boat as fast as my little skiff will go. See him drop a buoy and then my bow goes *wham!* into the side of the Whaler, and he falls down inside the boat. Cursing and hollering, madder than a bee in a jar.

Knocked me down, too, but I don't care. I'm glad I hit him, even if it probably did more damage to my boat than his.

"Tyler Croft, you're a thief! I hope you die, you miserable piece of crud!"

Tyler's head pokes up over the side and I can see him clear as day. He's smiling.

"Well, look who I bumped into," he says.

"I bumped into you."

"Whatever."

"You owe me five hundred dollars," I go, making up a number. "Pay up or else."

"Or else what?"

"You'll get arrested. You'll go to jail."

"You're cracked, lobster boy. Why would I go to jail?" He's having fun now, teasing me.

"Stole my lobster. Cut my buoys."

"Yeah? Prove it."

"Saw you with my own eyes."

"You didn't see anything. It's too dark. Nobody will believe anything you say. You're just a lying swamper and everybody knows it!"

The thing that makes me maddest of all, that makes

me feel like I swallowed a frog, is how right he is. My word against his. Lobster boy versus rich boy. You know who wins that fight. I ain't got money for lawyers and he does, or anyhow his father does.

No way can I win against him.

Our boats have started to drift apart. My motor has stalled, so I get out the oars and try to close the distance.

He sits there, waiting, like he's got nothing better to do than remind me that I can't hurt him but he can hurt me.

"Why'd you do it, Tyler?"

"Do what, Swamp Thing? Mess with your stupid traps?"

"Yes."

"Come a little closer, I'll tell you."

That makes me stop where I am, backing water.

Tyler stands up, swinging a boat hook. I duck and feel it whoosh over my head.

"You're a loser, lobster boy! Get used to losing!"

Then he fires up his big outboard and zooms away, rich boy in the dark of night, laughing and hooting my name, Skiff-eeeeee, Skiff-eeeeee.

My motor still won't start. I'd like to unhook the rotten old motor and drop it in the water, but I don't. Instead, I row all the way home.

Takes me the rest of the night. Night ain't half so dark as what's inside my brain.

13

When You Wake Up

WHEN I finally drag my tired butt into the house, it's four in the morning and my dad ain't on the TV couch, he's sitting at the kitchen table drinking coffee. Circles so dark around his eyes, he looks like a skinny raccoon with a dirty beard.

Wants to know where I been.

"What happened, Skiffy?"

"Nothin'. Motor wouldn't start."

But I can tell he knows that ain't the whole story. Figure it'll go faster if I say what happened. Then I can go to bed and sleep forever.

When I'm done telling, he looks as sick as me.

"The Croft kid has been cutting your traps? Why'd he do a thing like that?"

I shrug. "For the fun of it, I guess. And because I'm a swamper and he's not."

"Swamper? You serious? Didn't think anybody still used that word."

"Tyler does."

"I thought them days was long gone," says Dad, talking to himself. "I'll be darn."

"So," I say, "you gonna call Mr. Croft and make him pay for what Tyler done?"

Dad looks at the floor and sighs. He gets himself up from the chair, goes to the Frigidaire, and takes out a can of beer. He pops the tab and studies the foam. "I'll have to think about that," he says.

"You think about it," I tell him. "I'm going to bed."

There's a time just before you wake up when your brain thinks all the bad things that have happened only happened in your sleep. Wake up, your brain says, wake up and everything will be okay.

What a crock. When I wake up, all the bad stuff is still there. The *Mary Rose* still don't have an engine, and my traps are still cut.

Oh yeah, and my dad is passed out on the TV couch, which makes it perfect. I can smell the beer even before I get downstairs. I hate that smell. It comes from the pile of beer cans on the floor by the couch, and it comes from him, too. Passed out with his mouth open, like a little bird waiting for the next meal.

I kick that stupid pile of beer cans across the room, but he don't notice. I could set off a firecracker and he wouldn't notice, that's how drunk he is.

Looking at the scattered cans and the sight of him snoring with his mouth open, I decide I hate him almost as much as I hate Tyler Croft. 'Course I don't, not really, but it's one of those mornings where it feels good to hate somebody.

By the time I finish my cereal I'm done hating him for the time being, and I go in and clean up the cans and open a window to air out the smell.

Don't seem right that it's a beautiful summer day, with the sun shining to beat the band. I'd rather it was foggy and miserable, like me. I go out to check on *Rose,* but really, what's the point? Dad was right, should have left her sunk at the dock.

Thought I had it all sussed out, how to make the money for a new engine and all. What I didn't figure on was Tyler, and I should have. There's always some-body like him, looking to make folks miserable. Can't fight him no more than you can fight the wind or the tide. Wasn't him it would be somebody else. Joey Gleeson or Parker Beal. Somebody. My mom used to say there's always another turd in the bowl, no matter how hard you flush.

She was joking, but it's true.

For a while I mope around the *Mary Rose* and the dock. Check out my skiff, see there's a place on the bow needs fixing, from crunching into the Whaler, but I ain't in the mood. Finally I settle down and chuck around with the motor. Turns out it weren't nothing crucial, just a loose connection on the fuel line. So I start her and head up the creek for Mr. Woodwell's place.

Don't know why exactly, just to get away.

Something about the old man's boat shed always

calms me down. Like the air is quiet there, and when you breathe it, the quiet gets inside you. Smell of them cedar shavings is nice, too, or maybe it's the smell from Mr. Woodwell's corncob pipe. Anyhow, that's where I go, and when I get there, Captain Keelson's long rowing boat is at the dock.

The two of them are in the shed, studying a broken oar.

Mr. Woodwell looks up and goes, "'lo, Samuel! What are the fish doing today?"

"Swimming around, I guess."

Captain Keelson gives me his crinkly smile and says hello. "Broke an oar," he says. "Caught the blade on a piling."

Mr. Woodwell has the broken oar clamped in a vise on his bench. I can tell they're in no rush to fix it. They're at the talking-about-it stage and that will take awhile.

"*Rose* okay, is she?" the old man asks. "Still dry?"

I nod and pretend to study the oar, but the truth is, I can't tell where it broke.

"How about your lobster business?" Captain Keelson

asks. "Going pretty good, is it? Dev Murphy says you're catching 'em by the bushel."

"Dev Murphy don't know everything!" I say, feeling hot inside.

Now they're both studying me instead of the broken oar.

"Best tell us, Samuel," says the old man.

"Won't do no good."

He puffs his pipe and nods. "Come up the porch," he says. He turns to the captain. "Alex, you mind?"

"Amos, as you know very well, I don't care if that oar gets repaired this year or the next. I've plenty of oars."

The old man nods. "Boy needs a drink. Strong lemonade with plenty of sugar. Care to join us?"

We go up the porch and wait there while Mr. Woodwell fiddles in the kitchen, squeezing juice from the lemons.

"Weather's been good," the captain says, looking out on the creek.

"Yup. Pretty good."

"Remarkable lack of fog," he says.

"I guess."

"There was a summer when the sun never shined. This is before you were born. Fog came in on the Fourth of July and didn't leave until Labor Day."

"Oh yeah?"

"It was so damp, the mold complained. Several people dissolved. Just melted away in the street. Left nothing behind but soggy pairs of shoes."

I know he's trying to make me smile, but I ain't got one to spare.

"Fog was so thick, they were selling it by the slice. Genuine State of Maine Fog. Very popular with the tourists, if you could find one. Many got so lost, they ended up in Pennsylvania."

"That's pretty funny," I say, to be polite.

"Actually, Pennsylvania is a very serious state."

Mr. Woodwell brings out the steel pitcher and three glasses. "What did I interrupt?"

"Fog," says Captain Keelson.

"Fog? Alex does a mighty fine fog, if I do say so. Did you tell him about the man who melted?"

"I did."

"Left nothing behind but his hat."

"It was shoes," I tell him.

"Must have been another fellow."

"Thank you," I say when he hands me the icy glass.

Captain Keelson takes a sip and makes a face. "Didn't spare the lemons, did you, Amos?"

"Too tart?"

"No. Exactly tart enough. Thank you kindly."

"How about you, young man?"

"Really good," I say. "Like always."

Mr. Woodwell settles back in his rocker. His hands are so cramped up, he has to use both of 'em to hold the glass, but it don't seem to bother him. "Now then, Samuel," he goes. "You are among friends. Something is troubling you. If there's anything either of us can do to be of assistance, you have only to ask."

"There's nothing nobody can do."

"Just so you know."

"My traps been cut!"

"Good heavens!" says Captain Keelson, so surprised, he spills lemonade on his shirtfront. "How many?"

"Don't know, exactly. Most of 'em." Then I tell them the whole story, like I done with my dad. Except

I leave out the part where I smacked Tyler's Boston Whaler.

When I'm done, Captain Keelson sighs and goes, "He's correct, you know, Amos. There's very little we can do. It's an awkward situation. Big Skiff and Jack Croft have a history. Best not to meddle."

Mr. Woodwell nods in agreement, but he looks mournful sad. "I'm sorry, Samuel. I was thinking we might be able to help. But your father would not want us interfering in his personal affairs."

"It ain't my dad's problem. It's mine."

"Maybe so. But you're Big Skiff's son, and he's Jack Croft's son, and that makes it complicated. If anything is to be done, your father will have to do it."

'Course I knew that before I come up the creek. They made me tell for nothing, and that makes me mad all over again. Mad at Tyler and mad at my dad and mad at the beer cans on the floor and at myself for thinking it might be different.

"It's a sorrowful thing, that kind of cruelty," says Mr. Woodwell. "Not confined to boys, either."

"Mmm," says the captain. He leans forward and

catches my eye. "I suppose you'll try grappling for the lost traps?"

I ain't thought that far and he knows it. Real casual, he allows as how if I was to drag a grapple along the bottom, I might hook up on my traps.

"I guess," I say.

"You must be terribly discouraged."

"I'm mad is what I am. It ain't fair."

"No," says Mr. Woodwell.

"Indeed no," says the captain. "Decidedly not."

We sit awhile, drinking our lemonades, and nobody says much after that.

14

By Hook and by Crook

NEXT couple of weeks I work on finding my lost traps. Captain Keelson's idea about the grapple helps. What you do is tie the grapple — it's like a big fishhook with four barbs — to a length of rope. Then pull it along the bottom until it hooks on something. Might be a trap. Might be an old boot or a tire or a plastic milk crate or a clump of seaweed. All kinds of junk on the bottom.

Once I find this old telephone all clotted with mud. Take it to Dev Murphy at the bait house. He puts the receiver up to his ear and goes, "I hear the ocean!"

Sometimes if it's in a shallow spot and the water is flat calm, you can see the trap down there. Sometimes a lost trap comes up clicking with lobster. More often it don't.

Anyhow, I got nothing better to do. Stripers are running, but somehow it don't seem right, taking time off for fun. Not until I get the traps back. 'Course I can't locate them all. Tide or current has shifted 'em, or I don't recall exactly where I set 'em. Figure out of two hundred traps I'll get back half, eventual.

Dev thinks I should rig out and put them back in the water, but what's the point? I know Tyler. He won't quit on this. He come by in his Whaler to tell me so. Parker Beal is with him. Parker don't say nothing, he just tries to look tough, and laughs at everything Tyler says, like that's his job.

"Hey stinky!" Tyler shouts. Keeping well away in case I try to ram him with the skiff. "Whatcha doing, lobster boy?"

"What's it look like?"

"Looks like you're trolling for more stupid junk to put in your stupid junky shack. Drag long enough you'll probably find an old toilet seat for your outhouse."

Matter of fact, I had pulled up a toilet seat but threw it back. He must have seen me from the shore.

"Go away," I say. "Leave me alone."

"It must really suck being you, Skiffy. How do you stand it?"

"Come in a little closer, I'll tell you."

He laughs. Parker laughs, too, of course, but he don't know why exactly, except Tyler wants him to.

"Later, lobster boy!"

Then the Whaler zooms off. I'm still mad, but it's a deep mad now, not on the surface, so I can stand it without my ears getting hot whenever I think about what he done, and what he keeps on doing.

Sometimes I wonder why he hates me so. I never did nothing mean to Tyler, but he's always been at me, since back when his dad and my dad were friends. Got so miserable on the school bus, with him pulling my ears and singing that song he made up, that I took to riding my bike. My mom used to say he'd grow out of it, but he just grew meaner and meaner.

You ever seen where someone will take a magnifying glass and try to focus the sun on a fly until it burns? Just because they want to hurt something and they got nothing better to do?

Feels like Tyler is the sun and I'm the fly.

One day I'm going by the fish co-op when a big sport-fishing boat is unloading. Not *Fin Chaser* or I wouldn't have gone in close. Some fancy boat I never seen before. There's a whole crowd standing around and jawing, so I tie up to see what all the fuss is about.

"Will you look at that fish!" somebody says, and then whistles. "Four hundred and ten pounds!"

The boat captain has a big ice chest open and he's letting folks admire his fish. It's a giant bluefin tuna like my dad used to harpoon. Seven foot long and built for speed.

"Now that is a beautiful animal," the captain says, showing it off like a fancy sports car. "See the big tail? Bluefin can flick its tail back and forth thirty times a second. That's faster than the eye can see. Turbocharged thruster. See these dorsal fins? How they fold back into a groove? That decreases drag, increases efficiency. Even has special eyelids to make it move faster through the water. Gills have ram ventilators for increased oxygen. Strong, rapid heart for power. Warm-blooded, so it's quick. How quick? Bluefin can hit fifty miles an hour. It can leap fifteen feet into the air. It will swim two thousand miles to feed on a particular school of fish, at a particular time of year. When the good Lord created fish, He reached perfection with the bluefin tuna! This is the fish of all fishes. The king of fish! The queen of the Seven Seas!"

Folks are mighty impressed that he knows so much, but the captain — a tall, skinny guy with a sunburn — he laughs it off. "Don't get me wrong. I'm no expert. Got it all off the Internet! Easy as falling down."

"How many you catch so far this year?" someone asks.

"How many? Why, this is the first tuna I ever caught in my life."

"You serious?"

"Serious as a heart attack."

"How'd you hook it, then?"

"Pure luck," he admits. "I was bottom fishing for cod out near Jeffrey's Ledge when a whole school of tuna swam by, feeding on mackerel. Lucky I happened to have the big reel on board. Threw out a chunk of bait and *wham!* Hit it like a locomotive. All I did was hold on until it got tired. Fish did all the work."

He shows off the fancy rod and reel that whipped the fish.

"Nice. How much a rig like that cost?"

The captain shrugs, like he's embarrassed to mention the price. "These are expensive. Reel is a grand, rod five hundred. But worth every penny."

He's about ready to tell the story of catching the tuna all over again, for anybody who didn't hear it the first time, when Mr. Nagahachi the fish buyer shows up.

He's this short, stocky Japanese guy with shiny black hair and a big smile. I seen Mr. Nagahachi checking out tuna before, when my dad was fishing. What he does is make a couple of cuts to see the quality of the meat, and then he uses a little tool to take a sample of the fat content. That helps him set the price.

If he buys the fish he'll pack it in ice and send it overnight by air to Japan, for auction at the Tokyo fish market tomorrow.

Ten minutes later, Mr. Nagahachi tells the captain he'll buy the whole fish for sixteen dollars a pound, cash or certified check.

Six thousand five hundred and sixty dollars for one fish that got caught by accident!

Folks on the wharf are shaking their heads in amazement. Happens all the time, but it's still amazing that one fish can be worth so much just because people on the other side of the world like to eat little bits of it raw, on a mound of sticky rice.

"You know what it's like?" somebody says. "Like winning the lottery. Only more fun."

"Don't kid yourself, George," a friend of his says. "That boat cost half a million bucks if it cost a penny. And you heard how much he paid for the rod and reel."

The guy called George goes, "Who says you have to spend that much? You heard the man, he wasn't even looking for tuna. It came right up to his boat and asked to be caught. Think about it. That's like finding money on the sidewalk!"

"Why don't you do it, then, George? Get yourself a boat and hook up a tuna?"

"Maybe I will," says George. "Next year."

"I knew it," says his buddy, grinning. "All talk, no action."

I wait around until most of the crowd gets bored and goes away. Until Mr. Nagahachi has got the big tuna loaded into his van and packed in ice for the trip to the airport.

"'Scuze me," I go. "Can I ask you a question?"

He nods, looks like he's trying to place me.

"You pay that much for tuna tomorrow or the next day?" I ask.

"Depends on fish," he says. "Sometimes more, sometimes less."

"How much less?"

"Eight dollars a pound for skinny fish. Eighteen for nice fat fish."

"Thanks."

"Where's Big Skiff? You his son, am I right?"

"He's sort of retired for a while."

"Retire? He young man. Too young to retire. Big Skiff, he the best harpoon. Always strike good fat fish! Tell him I say 'hi,' okay?"

"Sure," I say. "I'll tell him."

I mean it, too. But when I get home, Dad is passed out on the couch with a whole new load of empty beer cans. Maybe he used to be the best, like everybody says, but right now he couldn't catch a tuna if it jumped in his lap.

But I'm thinking maybe I can.

15

Where the Big Fish Live

WHAT that tuna does, it gives me a whole new way of thinking. I been moping around and feeling sorry for myself, but maybe Tyler done me a favor. Work my butt off all summer hauling traps? Make money a dollar at a time? Why bother, when all I got to do is catch one measly tuna!

Okay, not measly, exactly. Has to be a big tuna. Five hundred pounder would be nice. Tuna get as big as a thousand pounds, but I ain't greedy. Five hundred will do. Then I'll have so much money, I can buy all kinds of stuff. First thing, the rebuilt motor for *Rose*. But I deserve a new bike, right? Fancy mountain bike

even better than Tyler's. And a new vacuum cleaner so the house don't get so dirty. New curtains for the windows, like Mom was planning on. Whatever we need, we'll get it.

Amazing, when you think about it. A bluefin tuna is going to change my life. Maybe change my dad's life, too. Wait till he hears that new motor purring in *Rose* — he'll want to get back fishing and acting like normal again. Me and him will be partners and a little pip-squeak like Tyler Croft won't dare cut Big Skiff Beaman's traps, no siree, not if he wants to live another day.

One fish, that's all it takes. One big fish!

I'm too excited to eat supper. Too many things to do. First is check out the line situation. There's a tub of heavy line in the bait shack that don't look too bad. I pull it out and walk it back and forth along the dock to measure it. Six hundred feet, more or less. Should be plenty.

Takes me an hour or so to coil it just so in the tub, the way I seen my dad do when he was harpooning tuna.

That's what I'm aiming to do, see. Harpoon me a

bluefin tuna! One that'll be so fat and juicy, it'll make Mr. Nagahachi reach for his wallet. One that's rolling around out there right this minute, waiting for me to show up. Big fish with my name on it. *Try and catch me, Skiff Beaman!*

Anyhow, first things first. Got the heavy line coiled in the plastic tub. Next thing, a keg to attach to the line. Because that's how they do it. You stick the tuna with a harpoon. The harpoon dart is tied to one end of a line and the keg to the other. Line runs out and the tuna pulls the keg around until it gets tired. Then you grab the keg and pull, and on the end of the rope is a big fish. Easy as falling down.

Takes me another hour or so to locate a keg that looks the right size. Not too big and not too small. Too big and the dart will pull out of the tuna. Too small and the tuna won't get tired quick enough. Heard Dad say that many times, back in the day. Gotta be exactly right, and there it is, the perfect keg, hiding behind the tool chest.

I drag the tub of line and the keg along the dock and lower it into my skiff. Haven't figured out what to do for a harpoon yet, but I will, eventual.

Next is fuel for the outboard. I grab a couple of empty gas cans and walk to the gas station and fill them up and walk back home. Round trip about a mile. Harder on the way back, with the gas cans yanking on my arms. Don't know how much gas I'll need, but more than usual, that's for sure. Takes two trips to fill the tanks. So there's another hour and a half gone.

Bait. I get my last bucket of salt herring from the cooler in the shack and put it under the middle seat in the skiff. Might come in handy if I need to put out a chum slick — bits of cut-up bait that put the smell of food in the water.

It's full dark by the time I go back in the kitchen and make a stack of peanut butter and jelly sandwiches and fill a jug of water. Provisions for the trip. I ain't hungry now, but sooner or later I will be, and a peanut butter and jelly sandwich always hits the spot.

After the food gets squared away, I check on my dad. Still passed out, or sleeping heavy. I turn off the TV and collect up the beer cans real quiet.

He rolls over, groans.

"Rose," he mutters, "that you?"

Moment later he's snoring away.

Part of me wants to leave him a note, let him know where I'm headed and what I intend to do. But the other part says don't be a fool. What if he wakes up in an hour and reads the note? He'll try and stop me for sure, or raise a fuss with the Coast Guard. Either way, no big fish. No big wad of cash money from Mr. Nagahachi. No rebuilt motor, no fancy mountain bike, no nothing.

Can't risk that.

I hang out by the dock until the tide goes slack. Time to move. I know what I need to do about the harpoon, but it's shameful, so I don't want to think about it. Just do it.

I'm about to untie the skiff and get going when I remember the compass. Never needed a compass hauling traps because I was always in sight of land. But going offshore in the dead of night is different. Got to know which way is east.

"Hey, Rose?" I go. "May I come aboard?"

The *Mary Rose* shifts a little as she takes my weight. I know a boat ain't really alive, not like a human being is alive. But sometimes it seems like the *Mary Rose* knows me almost as good as I know her.

"Rose, you mind if I borrow your compass for a little while? I promise to bring it back, good as new."

Rose don't mind. I unscrew the compass and take it back to the skiff and screw it down to the middle seat. Mighty big compass for a small boat. Compass like that you could steer all the way to Portugal. I ain't going near so far. Just thirty miles, more or less. Thirty miles seems like a mighty long way to go in a ten-foot skiff, but compared to Portugal it ain't much.

Thirty miles out to sea. Thirty miles to where the big fish live. Thirty miles to the end of the rainbow and the pot of gold. Thirty long miles in a very small boat, in the dark of night, alone.

Best get moving.

16

The Blushing Bandit

At the bend of the creek I shut off the outboard and get out the oars. Rowing soft and quiet as I come around the curve. Last thing I want is for Mr. Woodwell to see me. Not that he will. The lights are out in his house. Old man like him goes to bed early, I guess. Unless he's sitting on the porch in the dark.

Soon as I think about the porch I can feel him looking, wondering what I'm up to, coming in so sneaky. 'Course it's just my imagination — he's probably sound asleep and dreaming of the boats he made. Plus he can't see so good anyhow. Must be dead to the world by now. Stands to reason.

But just in case, I come up on the far side of the dock, out of sight from the porch. Nudge my skiff on the bank and stand ankle-deep in the cool water listening to the quiet. Even the birds gone to sleep. Only sound is crickets and peepers and the hush of warm summer wind.

I take a deep breath, ease it out.

There's a hot blush on my cheeks. Always happens when I'm about to do something bad. Once when I filched a cookie from the jar, Mom called me the Blushing Bandit, on account of my red face. You know what? Having her laugh at me was worse than getting spanked. Made the cookie taste like dirt. Then she grabbed me up and said something that made me feel better. I don't remember what exactly because I was only four, but knowing Mom, it was funny and sweet and sassy.

Mosquito lights on my neck. I squash it real quiet. Then I'm up the bank to the far side of the boat shed. Seems bigger in the dark. Big as a castle from a storybook. The high windows look like dark eyes watching me, and the shed doors are a giant mouth.

Tell myself, don't be stupid. It's a boat shed, that's all it is. An empty boat shed. Get a grip.

My head feels light with knowing what I got to do. Which is exciting and scary all at the same time. I slip up to the shed and lean against the outside wall. The boards are rough and smell of rain and old wood. Feel my way along the boards until I get to the big iron latch.

Here's where I got to be extra quiet. Mr. Woodwell may be halfway deaf, but a squeaky door will get inside your sleep. I ease up the latch and feel the weight of the big door. It wants to open and let me in. Big, old hinges don't squeak, they make a deeper sound like *ohhhh nooooo*. Or maybe like an old man clearing his throat.

I slip inside and pull the door shut. Take another deep breath and taste the smell of fresh wood shavings. Kind of a green smell that feels good inside your nose and down the back of your throat, like spearmint candy.

At first it's so dark in the boat shed, it's like a soft blanket settled over my eyes. Then I can make out the shape of the high windows and a smudge of starlight. Still can't see much, but enough to make out the farthest wall. On the way I stub my toe on a sawhorse, but manage to swallow the ouch.

Serves me right, sneaking in like a thief.

Try to tell myself what I got in mind ain't stealing exactly. But if it ain't stealing, what is it?

Feel along the back wall. Finding tools hung on pegs, splinters, knotholes. What I'm after is out of reach, so I drag over a sawhorse and climb up on it. Kind of holding my breath as I reach up.

There it is, right at my fingertips. My father's harpoon. The one he made and gave to Mr. Woodwell. I lift it off the pegs, expecting heavy, but the harpoon is light. Long and light and balanced where you hold it. The surprise of that makes me dizzy, I guess, because the next thing I'm on my back in the sawdust and I can't breathe. Got the wind knocked all the way out and it takes awhile to get it back, a little at a time.

When I'm breathing again I worry some more about Mr. Woodwell. What'll he say if he finds me taking his harpoon? What'll I say back? Can't think of nothing that makes it right, but that don't stop me doing it. I been over it in my own head and there's no way around it. The fish are out there right now. Tomorrow or the next day might be too late. So I got to head out tonight and be there when the sun comes up, ready to strike the first big fish that rises. Need a harpoon for that, no two ways about it.

It's not like I can ask to borrow the harpoon. Tell the old man I'm headed out to the tuna fishing grounds and he'll rope me to a chair and call my dad, or worse. So I tell myself Mr. Woodwell will understand after it's over. After I got my fish and the money and everything. But mostly I try not think about how wrong it is, stealing from Mr. Woodwell, who's been so good to me.

In the end he don't wake up, or anyhow he don't come out to the shed to see what's making all the noise falling down and squeaking the doors.

First thing I notice outside the shed is a swarm of lightning bugs shining like little stars in the tall grass. Like they're pointing the way back to my skiff. Figure that has to be a good sign, when the bugs want to help you find your way.

I scurry down the bank to where my skiff is waiting.

The harpoon is longer than the boat. So long, it sticks out over the bow like the emblem on an old car. Big old harpoon is meant to be used, ain't it? What's the point of making a thing like that if it never gets used?

Once I'm out on the creek I stop worrying about Mr. Woodwell and start thinking about the giant fish. The big bluefin. I can almost hear it talking. Sassing me like a bully in the schoolyard. *Come and get me, lobster boy. Come and get me if you dare.*

17

Three Rules for Skiff Beaman

DOWN the creek I go, with the dark all around and the trees watching and the water shining black. Down the creek and past our little house, where my dad is passed out on the TV couch. Down the creek to the river, where the current is fast and the water is deep. Down to the river and out to the harbor, where the lighthouse stands on a hunk of bare rock, tall as a giant with a head of light.

The only sounds are the slap of water on the hull and the mutter-putter of the outboard motor. And me whistling soft to keep myself company.

At this time of night my skiff is the only boat on the move. All the other boats in Spinney Cove are sleeping at their moorings. I'm wondering if the bluefin tuna sleep, too. Some fish sleep, others got to keep moving. Probably your big blue is the keep-moving kind.

Once I asked my dad how fish see way down deep where it's always dark. He told me a fish has got special nerves under its skin so it can feel the shape of things moving in the water. Little fish twitches, the big fish feels it, good as we can see with our eyes. You mean like magic, I asked, and he thought about that and said, no, it's not magic, it's just Nature's way to give one creature advantage over another.

That's when Mom chimed in to say the main advantage of being human is the brain, so use it or lose it, young man. She was big on that, wanting me to think about things, and do good in school, and read books and stuff. Sometimes in the middle of my head I can still hear her going, "Show the world what you're made of, Skiff Beaman."

Couldn't hardly get through the kitchen without her saying that. Or reminding me what the three rules were. Mom's Three Rules. Rule Number One, think smart. Rule Number Two, speak true. Rule Number Three, never give up. First two I'm always forgetting. The third one, that's why I'm out here. Only thing, what if never giving up means not thinking smart or speaking true? Does it cancel out?

God gave you a brain, Skiff Beaman. Use it.

Okay, Mom. I'm trying. Honest.

Honest? You just stole a harpoon from that nice old man!

Had to, Mom. Can't give up, remember? Rule Three.

You smart-mouthing me, Skiff Beaman?

No, ma'am.

All right, then. Can't change what's already been done. But you be careful.

I'll be careful.

You know where you're going, and how to get there?

Yes, ma'am.

Stay in the boat. Whatever happens, you stay in the boat. Promise?

Yes, Mom. I promise.

Tide carries me past the lighthouse.

Put the light behind you and steer for the big red buoy.

My dad said that the first time he ever took me out in the *Mary Rose*. Sat me on his lap and let me steer for the buoy. He was always doing that, explaining which way to go, what rocks to stay clear of, and where the channel markers were. So I know which way to go, once I clear the harbor. Flat east for thirty miles. Couldn't be simpler. Just head into the sunrise, that's where the fish are waiting. Piece of cake. Any fool can find the Ledge. Why not me?

When I pass the big red buoy it sighs at me. That's just air going up and down inside as it rides on the swell. But it almost sounds human, and mournful, like it thinks I'm making a big mistake. Maybe I am. But I can't stop now. No way. For the rest of my life I'd be sick thinking on what might have been. Sick on missing my big chance.

Think fish, I tell myself. Don't think about how big the dark is, or how small the skiff feels, or how scared you are. Scared from the inside out, from the pit of your stomach to the tips of your fingers. The kind of scared that makes you tingle all over.

Think fish. Big fish shining like a lighthouse, showing you the way. Big fish gonna change your life.

Big fish, big fish.

Thinking on that big fish so hard, I almost forget to check the compass. Lucky for me it glows in the dark, and I line up the "E" and stick to it.

Trust your compass. That's another thing my dad was always saying. Trust your compass because you can't trust your instincts in the dark or the fog. Without a compass a man will steer himself in a circle, nine times out of ten. Give up on the compass and you're lost for sure.

Every once in a while I look back, and each time the lighthouse beacon gets smaller and fainter. After a while it's only a glow on the edge of night. Then comes a time it ain't there at all. Which means I've gone at least five miles. Five miles out to sea.

Twenty-five miles to go. Should take three, maybe four hours.

Nothing to it. Piece of cake. Nothing to be scared of, so long as I stay in the boat and trust the compass.

Still, I keep thinking how much water there is. Black, black water. Water so dark and deep, it takes your breath away. Water so everywhere and all around, you can't tell it from the sky, or the sky from the water, or whether you're rising or falling.

Don't think about that. What does it matter how deep the water is? Think about steering east. Think about getting there. Think about big fish. Think about what you'll do with the money. Think about the *Mary Rose* as good as new, and your dad as good as new, too, and Tyler Croft with the outhouse song dying in his stupid throat.

Steer east.

Steer east.

Steer east and think about what happens when the sun comes up and the big fish rises.

I'm steering east and pretty much over being scared to death when the motor up and quits.

18

What Happened
to the Stars

NOTHING like a quit motor to put a lump in your throat. I got so used to the sound of it that the sudden quiet almost hurts.

Ain't just the quiet, though. Without a motor to push a boat along, the sea takes over and does what it wants. Soon as the motor quits, the big swells start to turn the skiff around. Turning me like the wind turns a leaf in a puddle, making the compass spin from east to west and round again. Feels like I'm going down the drain.

This is bad, real bad.

I yank on the cord. The motor sputters and dies.

Yank again and again. Nothing. What went wrong? Could be a hundred things. Bad spark plug. A broken wire. A gummed-up carburetor. Maybe the miserable old motor finally died of old age — and no way to know for sure in the dark.

I'm so mad and scared, I almost cry. Almost but not quite. Finally I think to check the gas tank, which I should have done right away. It's bone dry! I switch the fuel hose over to the next tank, squeeze the primer bulb, and yank on the starter cord, thinking, pleasepleaseplease start.

The old outboard sputters to life.

Sweetness! Nothing sounds so pure and sweet as a motor running when you're all alone in the middle of nowhere. Minute later I've got the skiff headed east again. East for the Ledge. East until the sun comes up. East where the big fish live.

I look up, hoping to see the stars, but there must be clouds because the sky is as black as the sea.

Nothing to do but trust the compass.

You sure this is a good idea, Skiff Beaman?
I don't know. But it's the only idea I got.

Rule Number Three doesn't mean risk your life. It never meant that.

Don't worry, Mom, I'll stay in the boat.

When you were little you were scared of the dark.

Still am. Don't matter.

Had to leave the night-light on or you'd wake up crying.

That's when I was a baby.

Remember what I told you: Being brave isn't the same as being stupid.

I'm not being brave. I'm just going fishing.

Be careful, Skiffy dear. That harpoon is bigger than you are.

I'll be careful, Mom. I won't do nothing stupid.

It's not like I think my mom is really talking to me. More like all the things she said are stored inside my brain and come out when I'm alone. Like I know what she'd say about stuff, and how she felt about things, and what she'd want me to do.

Once when I was about six I did a cannonball off the dock. The water was way over my head and Dad had to fish me out or I might've drowned. After they dried me off, Mom asked what was I thinking, to do such a thing? I told her I was learning how to be brave. That's when she said that thing about brave not being the same as stupid, and that before I could try being brave I had to use my brain and be smart.

Life is a gift, she said, whenever I did something really dumb, like ride my bike no hands with my eyes closed down Spotter Hill on a dare. Life is a gift and you mustn't just throw it away.

So here I am in the middle of the Atlantic Ocean, thinking about my mom and praying on the sun to come up soon. Thinking everything will be okay when the sun comes up. When the sun comes up there will be other boats out fishing for giant tuna, same as me. Get in trouble, all you got to do is wave your arms or make some noise, they'll lend a hand.

Once when my dad was out on the *Mary Rose* a storm come on sudden, and the swells broke out in whitecaps and he decided to head in early, just to be cautious. Then a cooling hose blew and he lost power and started to take on water. Dev Murphy saw him and towed him home, which ain't easy in a heavy sea. Both boats got beat up by the storm, with windows broke and gear smashed and traps lost overboard. When I asked Dad if he had to pay Dev back he said that's not how it works. Fish and you fish alone, every man for himself. But when one man gets in trouble at sea we're all in trouble. We're in it together, so you lend a hand and don't think of what it costs, because the next time it might be you with a busted motor or a sinking boat and the waves crashing all around.

Not a soul out here with me at the moment, though. Not even a bird in the sky. Ain't really a sky you can make out, more a close-up darkness right over my head. Just me and my skiff and the sound of the motor putt-putting along, and the slap of black water on the hull.

After a time the steep swells smooth out. Nothing to see but the compass. Keep the arrow on the big "E" for east, I know that much. Now and then I flick the flashlight beam out from the skiff, but it don't catch nothing but water. Water so black, it sucks up the light.

If you think you're alone, try singing a song. Somebody's sure to tell you to shut up.

Not much for singing, Mom. Not like you.

I won't laugh, Skiffy, promise. Go on and sing.

Can't think of a song right now.

Sure you can. Remember your favorite song when you were five years old? The fishing song?

I do remember that song, or part of it, anyway. *Momma's going fishing, papa's going fishing, I'm a going fishing, too.* Dad bought me a brand-new pole for my birthday but wouldn't give it to me until I learned that song. Trouble was, once I learned it I wouldn't shut up. Sang that silly song until Mom said if I sang it one more time her ears would fall off. You promise? I said, because I thought ears falling off was pretty cool, and she got to laughing so hard, Dad had to pat her on the back. Sing it all you want, she said when she got done laughing. Sing it until it wears you out. What about your ears? I asked. I like my ears, she said, touching the earrings Dad gave her for their anniversary. I like my ears and I think I'll keep 'em. Now you go on and sing.

My voice sounds real small against the empty all around, but it feels good singing. Let the ocean know I'm here.

"Momma's going fishing. Papa's going fishing. I'm a going fishing, too."

Sounds better if I hit the seat with my hand, keeping the rhythm. *Wompa, wompa, wompa.*

"Momma's going fishing! Papa's going fishing! I'm a going fishing, too!"

Trouble is, all I can remember is just that one line of the song. There's something about a cane pole and a fishing hole, but I can't find it. So it's just as well there's no one to hear me acting stupid. Boy in a small boat singing his head off, can't even recall the whole stupid song. Probably think being all alone in the dark made me crazy or something.

Maybe I am. Crazy, I mean. What a totally insane idea, take a boat this small offshore this far! What was I thinking? Even when the sun does come up I won't be able to see land. How will I ever find my way back home?

The compass, you fool. Stop your blubbering! You got a compass, don't you? A good, solid compass from the *Mary Rose*. A compass that always got her home, even in the worst kind of weather. Catch your fish, Skiff Beaman, then head west. Head west for long enough and you'll bump into land. Might not be the harbor at Spinney Cove, if the current sets against you, but it will be land. Sell that big tuna to Mr. Nagahachi and you can take a limousine home.

Me in a limousine. The idea makes me laugh, and somehow that gets me off worrying myself to death. Shake my head to clear it and realize I been drenched in cold sweat. Soaked through to my skin. Or that's what I think at first. Only I can feel the wet in the air as I putt along. It ain't me that's in a cold sweat, it's the dark itself.

Fog.

That's what happened to the stars, you knucklehead. Fog so thick, it melts on your face. Bad fog. Blind fog. White darkness. What they call a real peasouper.

All I can do is pray for sunrise. Pray the sun will burn off the fog and let me see again. Because if there's one thing scares me more than being lost in the dark, it's being lost in the fog.

19

If Mist Made the World

THE sun comes up, eventual. It always does, don't it?
No matter how much we fret and worry the night
won't end, the sun comes up. But this time the sun
don't touch the fog. Too thick for that. Fog so thick,
you can't see the sun, only the light it makes. Kind of
a dull white glow inside the mist.

My dad says fog is just a cloud that comes down to
eye-level. But clouds are fluffy and pretty and fog ain't
none of that. Fog is not being able to see where you're
going, or which way the waves are breaking. Fog
plays tricks with your eyes. Shows you shapes of
things that can't be there. A floating castle. A pirate

ship about to run you down. Monster things from your worst nightmare.

When I was little I somehow got it fixed in my head that fog came from dragons. Must have seen it in a book, fire-breathing dragons, only I got it wrong and thought the dragons were breathing fog. Dragons that had scales like fish, and breath that smelled of seaweed. There's still part of me believes that when fog comes in on the tide it means there's a dragon waiting inside the mist. A dragon that will suck you into the fog so hard, you'll never get out.

Stop it, fool! Stop fussing about imaginary monsters and stuff you can't touch. So you're fogged in, so what? You can still see your boat and the water around it, can't you? You can see farther than you can throw that big harpoon, that's for sure. What more do you need?

Birds, I'm thinking. I need birds. Birds is how you find fish. When fish make a commotion feeding on the surface, birds will circle over and dive. You can see the birds from a long ways off and know where the fish are. My dad says that's how the first human caught a fish, by watching what the birds did.

How can you spot birds in fog this thick? You can't. Plain and simple can't.

After a while I stop fretting and settle down. Can't do nothing about fog. It happens. You got to go with what you got. I got a good little skiff and a pail of bait and a finest-kind harpoon. Probably the first human had nothing but a sharpened stick or a piece of rock. So I'm way ahead, right?

Right?

Shut up and fish. Saw a tourist with that on his T-shirt once. Makes sense. Now or never, I'm thinking. So I pry the lid off the bait bucket and cut up some herring and drop it over the side. Cutting it fine so the fish oil will spread. The idea is, attract small fish into the chum slick and the big fish will rise up to feed on the small fish. Sometimes it works and sometimes it don't and you never know until you try.

So I get to work, chopping and cutting. Fog? What fog? Oh *that* fog. Does it bother you? Heavens no. Love the fog. Hope it stays forever. You hear that, Mr. Fog? Stick around and see what happens.

I'm cutting up herring and dropping it over the side for most of an hour before I hear the first little splash.

Splash like a pebble makes. Figure it must be my imagination, but then there's another little *sploink!* And then a bunch more, like rain on a puddle.

Come on, fish! Over here. Feed your way up the chum slick, all the way to my boat.

Minute later, there it is. The nervous, zaggedy shape of a mackerel just beneath the surface, working the chum slick. Small mackerel, what we call tinker size. Maybe five inches long. Then another and another until there's a whole school of tinker mackerel darting up to nibble on the chum, fighting one another for the pieces I been cutting up and dropping into the water.

I'm grinning so hard, my face hurts. It's working! And tinker means I must be pretty near the Ledge, where the big fish come to feed. Got the mackerel in my slick, come on big tuna! Come on and take a bite. Show me your fin and I'll show you my harpoon.

Only trouble is, I got just one bucket of herring. One bucket, that's all I had room for, and already it's halfway gone. So I start cutting even smaller, and putting less pieces in the water. Barely enough to keep the slick water shining with fish oil. The tinker don't seem to mind, not at first. They're having a fine time swarming in the slick, darting around like small, speckled rockets. Grabbing bits of herring and shaking it like dogs with a bone.

"Hey, little fish. Stick around for the big fish, why don't you?" Bad habit of mine, talking out loud to fish. Makes it less lonesome, hearing the sound of my own voice. "Come over this way, Mr. Mackerel, you missed a piece. Ooh, don't let the bad boys get it! Fight for what's yours! Go on and eat it before somebody else does, or before something bigger eats you. Good. Here's another piece. More you eat, the bigger you'll grow. Bigger you grow, the better your chance."

Try to pick out one particular fish for a conversation, but they're swarming, so I keep losing 'em in the crowd. Can't tell one from another. Which makes you wonder, can they tell themselves apart or do they think all together? Are there bully fish that take advantage, and weaker fish that keep losing out? Must be. That's the way it is with most creatures, from what I can see. Birds, dogs, cats, and people, too. Which means there's nothing original about Tyler Croft. He comes from a long line that goes all the way back to the mean molecule. Mean old Tyler ever heard me talking to fish, he'd have himself a good laugh.

"Hey you! Psst. Yes, you. Funny-looking one with the pale spots." I flick a little chopped herring on the water and watch it settle. Watch the skittish fish watching me, watching the chum, trying to decide what to do, eat it or run away. "That's lunch," I tell 'em. "Don't worry about the bill, lunch is on me."

Fish scoots in, inhales the speck of chum. Fish scoots back into the school. Back behind the boat. Getting farther from the boat because I'm running out of chum. Trying to stretch it out, give the tinker just enough to stay in the vicinity and not a speck more.

Come on, Mr. Bluefin. Can't you smell the chum? Can't you feel the baitfish feeding? Ain't you hungry?

Tinker stay in the slick for an hour or more and then blink! They're gone, just like that. Like somebody flicked a switch.

Gone. And with 'em any hope of finding a big tuna.

I sit there inside the fog and curse myself for a fool. What was I thinking, bringing only one bucket of bait? Did I really think it would be that easy? Was I thinking at all?

Answer: Mostly I was thinking about the money I'd get for the fish instead of how to get the fish in the first place. Like if I could only get out to the Ledge, it would happen automatic. As if a hundred boats didn't go out every day and come back empty. Big, fancy boats with thousand-dollar trolling rods and gold-plated reels and radar and radios and fancy fish-finders and gallons of frozen chum. If boats like that come back empty, what can you expect from a plywood skiff with one pitiful bucket of salted herring for bait?

Nothing, that's what. And nothing is what I got.

So there I am, drifting in a world made of white mist and feeling mighty sorry for myself when all of a sudden I hear a splash. Not a little tinker-size splash.

A big splash.

20

Take My Breath Away

FIRST thing I do is grab the harpoon and stand up in the stern of the skiff. Trying to balance myself and the harpoon and keep my heart from pounding so hard, it makes my ears hot. All because of that splash. Sound of a giant bluefin tuna crashing into the water. What else could it be?

"Come on, fish," I whisper.

But that's all. Just the one splash, then nothing for the longest time. Harpoon starts feeling heavy, so I rest it on my shoulder and try to breathe normal. Listening hard, but I can't hear nothing but the slurp of water around the skiff.

Maybe I imagined that big splash out there behind the fog. Maybe I wanted to hear it so bad, my brain obliged. Or it was the fog playing tricks on my ears. Sometimes the fog makes a faraway noise seem close by. Hear a man talking and you think he's right next to you but really he's on the other side of the cove, clear across the harbor. So maybe the big splash came from miles away.

Maybe.

Then the fog gets bright and I realize it ain't my heart making my ears hot, it's the sun. Sun shining down through the fog, burning a hot blue hole in the sky. Sunlight never felt so good. Sun hits the white mist and the mist starts to get thin and wispy and then a little breeze stirs and the wall of fog starts to back away and I can see a fair distance, as much as a half mile or so.

Sea don't seem so empty with the sunlight making it look almost alive. Then I see it ain't just the sunlight glittering on the water. Something is happening back there in the last of my chum slick. A rippling just below the surface, like something is trying to get out.

My brain starts clicking. Should I put down the

harpoon and start the motor and steer toward the ripple? Or would the noise of the motor spook whatever it is? Before I can decide, a whole bunch of tinker mackerel explode from the water and scatter in all directions. Looks like a fountain of fish, hot and silver in the sunlight.

These tinker ain't feeding. No sir, these tinker are on the menu. Because before the little fish can get back underwater, a huge tuna comes up behind them and launches itself into the air like a fish-seeking missile.

A giant bluefin!

The big tuna hangs in the air long enough to catch the sunlight and then *wham!* back into the water with a mouthful of the little fish.

Never really knew what they meant by "take your breath away." Now I do. That big fish takes my breath away and he won't give it back. Whew! I come thirty miles in the dark and fog for this. Giant tuna going airborne. Heard all them stories my dad used to tell, about five-hundred-pound fish flying ten feet into air, like they were launched from a cannon. Big fish that can leap clean over a boat. Giant fish that think they can fly. Fish in such a frenzy to feed, they don't notice a man with a harpoon.

It's all true.

Then, much closer, a pale streak underwater. Slant of light catching a big fish ten or fifteen feet below the surface, streaking like a torpedo, so fast that the eye can't hardly keep up. Half-moon curve of the tuna's tailfin is nothing but a blur, accelerating from zero to fifty in a heartbeat. Makes me wonder how I'll ever get a harpoon into a thing that moves so fast.

Bluefin must be reading my mind, because one comes out of the water much closer to the boat — blue and silver and dripping in the sunlight — but it's back in the water and going deep before I can think to lift the harpoon, let alone throw it.

You got to be ready, but how do you know where the next one will come up? There! Another big bluefin whooshing along the surface like a speedboat, throwing a wake, chomping on tinker. Looks pretty close, so I heave the harpoon and pray for a strike.

Pitiful throw. Harpoon goes sideways and sort of doinks into the water. Misses by a mile. Meantime I fall across the stern and crack my elbow. When my elbow stops throbbing I pull on the line and draw the harpoon back to the boat. Tuna must be having a good laugh. You see that? Stupid kid can't throw worth beans.

Hard to believe my dad once harpooned eight of these amazing critters in a single day. Eight in one day! They still talk about it down the harbor, the time Big Skiff got eight fins and bought himself a pickup truck and a gold necklace for his wife and a bike for his boy, all with cash money.

When the line is coiled I stand up again, holding the harpoon shoulder high. Looking for the streaks in the water, trying to figure where a fish will come up, hoping it will be close enough to hit. I take another throw and this one is better but it still misses. Or maybe I was throwing at a shadow, hard to say. Tinker mackerel exploding like hard rain all around, but the bluefin are deeper now, driving the tinker up. Working together, half a dozen big tuna, keeping the little fish in a big ball so they can slash in and feed from underneath.

Part of me wants to put the harpoon down and just watch. Other part of me wants a big bluefin so bad, I can taste blood in my mouth. I know from how my dad used to talk that he mostly hit the fish when they were directly under him. More or less straight down. But none of these want to cooperate. Like they know how far I can throw and they stay that far away. Slashing at the poor tinker like they ain't eaten in months, like they're afraid they'll never eat again.

I use the oars to turn the skiff around so I can stand in the bow, which makes it easier to throw and not get tangled up in the rope. I'm holding the harpoon high, checking for streaks under the boat. Watching the amazing fish leap and slash dive and basically go nuts just out of range. Once I see a streak, but it's gone before I can even think to throw and by then it's too late.

I keep throwing anyhow, even when I can't see anything. Hoping luck will put a fish on the end of the harpoon. Harpooner has to be good, but his best friend is luck, that's what Dad used to say. Can't stick a fish without luck on your side.

I throw until I can't throw no more. Until my arm is all knotted up and aching and I ain't got the strength to lift the harpoon to my shoulder.

It's like the bluefin know how tired I am, because

they give one last flurry of feeding, making tinker explode in all directions, and then suddenly they're gone. It's amazing how fast it happens. One second they're everywhere, the next the sea goes flat quiet and it's like the fish were never there at all. Like I dreamed the whole thing.

More like a nightmare than a dream. Seeing all those big fish and not being able to hit one. The excitement drains out of me all at once. Like I'm on an elevator going down, down. What do I do now? Can't think. Like the mist has invaded my brain and made everything foggy inside my head.

Okay, first thing you do is sit down before you fall down. There, I'm sitting, what next? You're thirsty, right? So drink. Lift the water jug up to your mouth and drink. Good. That wasn't so hard, was it? Okay, what's next? You eaten lately? No? What about all those peanut butter and jelly sandwiches you brung along? Good idea. Only my hands are shaking so bad, I can hardly open the bag of sandwiches. Partly the shaking is because I'm so hungry. Didn't realize it until my brain said "food" and then all at once I'm starving.

I wolf down two sandwiches and the shaking stops. Think about eating a third sandwich but decide it's better to save it for later. Might be here awhile. Who knows when the big fish will come back. Or if they'll come back. Fog clears from my head a little and I'm thinking it was really stupid to keep throwing the harpoon even when the fish were out of range. Smarter to wait until you can't miss, even if that means waiting for hours. All throwing did was make my arm hurt and spook the fish. You got to choose your moment. That's something Dad used to say, but until now I never knew what it meant, exactly.

Full stomach makes me sleepy. I decide to take a little catnap while I got the chance. Might as well. Fish come back, the noise'll wake me up better than an alarm clock. So I lie down in the skiff and pull my cap down over my eyes and use my life jacket for a pillow.

I'm back home on the dock. Fog is so thick, I can't see the house. I can hear my mom and dad talking to each other but I can't see them. They're looking for me, but for some reason I can't make any noise. Can't make noise because I'm asleep, which don't make sense. Somehow I know I'm asleep in a dream, but it don't matter, I can't make noise and I can't wake up and I can't see Mom or Dad or the house. Want to call out to Mom worse than anything, but I can't. Like I'm tied down with soft ropes of fog or something and the fog has got inside my mouth and sucked all the talk right out of me.

Mom, I want to say, Dad, I'm over here. Keep looking and you'll find me. But their voices get farther and farther away and it's just me alone inside the fog and I can't move or talk and then Mom's voice turns into a horn and I wake up.

Blaaaaaat. Blaaaaaat. Blaaaaaat.

Foghorn. Something coming my way.

21

When the Whoosh Comes By

WHEN you hear a foghorn you're supposed to signal back. That way the other boat gets an idea where you are and steers away. Trouble is, I never thought to bring along a horn. Didn't even think there might be fog, which is really dumb because I know better. Maybe that's what the dream was telling me about not having a voice. Don't matter now, there's nothing I can do but listen.

Blaaaaaat.

Big old foghorn seems to be getting closer. I can hear a boat engine thumping. Then it seems to be going away and the engine gets fainter and fainter and the horn sounds smaller and then the wake comes through and rocks me like a baby in a cradle and I'm alone again inside the fog.

"How long did you sleep, you reckon?"

That's me talking out loud to myself. Got no good answer because another thing I forgot to bring along is a wristwatch. Figured I'd know what time of day it was from the sun, but the fog has come on thick again and I can't tell where the sun is, except it feels like I slept for a long time, so it might be afternoon now.

"Skiff Beaman, you are a darn fool."

There. Almost feels good to say it. To speak the truth out loud. Only a darn fool would do what I did. Go to sea in a ten-foot plywood skiff without a thought in my head but catch-a-big-fish. Like there was no room in my brain for what happens if there's fog, or you can't find the fish, or you can't hit the fish even if you find them. Turns out I found the fish all right, but it don't matter because I'm not big enough or strong enough to hit one with the harpoon. So here I am thirty miles out to sea in a blind fog with nothing but a few peanut butter and jelly sandwiches and a jug of water. Oh, and a compass in case I decide to give up and go home. Which I ain't ready for, not yet.

Why bother? Home is Dad on the TV couch and a boat with no engine and a rich kid laughing while he cuts my traps. Home is where my mom don't live anymore except she's still there somehow, in all the rooms of our little house, me and my dad missing her something fierce and not wanting to give up how much it hurts because that would be like forgetting. Home is a rickety old dock and an outhouse with a half-moon cut in the door, and the bright orange flowers my mom called "outhouse lilies." Home is where everything happens, good or bad, except it's been mostly bad lately.

So I'm lying there in the bottom of my little skiff, munching on a sticky sandwich and feeling sorry for myself when the whoosh comes by.

Whoosh.

There it is again. Sound of something slicing through the water. Not far away, either. Right on the other side of the plywood hull, a few feet from my head.

Whoosh.

Careful, I tell myself. Sit up slow. Don't rock the boat. Don't scare away whatever it is that's making that sound.

I sit up real slow. And see the tip of a fin over the top edge of the boat. Fin like the curved edge of a knife. A fin as blue as the sky on a perfect day in May. Big blue fin making the whoosh as a giant fish circles my boat.

Harpoon is lying along the seats with the tip out over the bow. I know what I want to do, but can I do it? Got to try. Now or never. No mistakes allowed.

I take the harpoon in my right hand while I'm still sitting down, facing the back of the boat. Keep hold of it while I ever so quiet stand up and turn around and face the front. Quiet now, quiet as a mouse. I stand on the seat without making a sound and look over the side into the dark, wet eye of a giant bluefin tuna, close enough to touch, and so alive, I swear I can hear his heart beating.

I'm looking down on the biggest fish I ever seen in my life. Bigger than me. Bigger than my boat. Bigger than any tuna I ever seen brought into the dock.

I got the harpoon raised but I don't dare move, not until it's perfect, not until I'm ready to strike.

I swear the giant fish is looking at the boat. Like maybe it wants to know if this is where the chum comes from that brings the mackerel it likes to eat. Can it still pick up on the scent of the bait I was cutting up and tossing over? Is that it? What's it thinking? Why is it circling my boat? Or is it circling me? Curious about a small boy with a long stick in his hand.

I never realized how much bigger a bluefin tuna looks when it's alive in the ocean instead of dead on the dock. I can feel the power as it swims by, making the boat rock with the *whoosh-whoosh-whoosh* of its giant tail shoving it through the water easy as can be. Man on the dock said the tail can move faster than the eye can see, but this one is going slow, gliding along as easy as can be. Almost like it's showing off. *Look at me, you puny human. Look at my big bad self, you never seen nothing so awesome as me.*

The big bluefin is so amazing and so beautiful, I almost forget what I need to do. Almost but not quite. My dad used to call it "getting froze up." Man out in the pulpit of a tuna boat, he's waiting for hours for a chance to throw and when the chance finally comes, he can't do it. Like the fish sort of hypnotizes you into not throwing the harpoon.

Froze up. Come to think of it, that's sort of what happened to Dad when Mom died. Except he ain't on a tuna boat, he's on the TV couch. Stuck on how miserable he feels.

Never mind your father and the couch, Skiffy. Concentrate on the fish!

She's right. There's plenty of time to worry about my dad later. So I wrap both hands around the shaft of the harpoon and plunge it straight down at the biggest part of the fish. Straight down with all my might. Straight down so hard and fast, I fall halfway out of the boat and my face is an inch from the water and I'm looking down and I don't see nothing.

Fish disappeared. Gone in the blink of an eye.

Had my chance and missed. Again.

I groan and roll over and rub my knee where I bumped it and then I fetch the harpoon and pull it into the boat. That's when I notice the barb is missing. Must have come loose when I fell down. Great. Harpoon without a barb is just a long stick. Then I remember the barb is attached to the keg line, so all I got to do is pull the line in and put the barb back on the harpoon.

Who knows? If I drift around for another hundred years or so, I might find another fish as big as the one that got away. Anyhow, I put my hand on the line and give it a tug and then a weird thing happens. The line slips through my hands.

Line is running out of the tub, over the side of the boat, and straight down into the water.

For a moment I can't make my brain figure out what that means, line running out of the boat, and then I stand up and shout, "FISH ON! FISH ON!" at the top of my lungs.

Nobody around to hear me, so it's like I'm shouting to myself, to make me believe what happened. I hit the big fish! He's got the barb in his back and he's diving deep, dragging line out of the tub. I'm so excited, I fall down again and crack another shin but I don't even care that it hurts because I got a fish on the line.

My dad used to talk about the first dive a bluefin makes after it gets hit. They call it "sounding." Most often a fish will go right to the bottom and stay there

for a while, until it figures out what happened. Sometimes a fish will run right across the surface, skipping
and leaping and trying to shake the barb loose. Other
times a fish will give up and die right away, if the barb
got buried deep enough.

My fish hasn't quit, not yet. Line's whipping out
like he's running clear across the ocean. Already the
tub is more than halfway empty and the line is still
running. I'm staring at it, trying to figure the best time
to throw the keg over the side. Wanting to check the
knot that holds the line to the keg, but I don't dare,
there isn't time; whatever knot I tied will either hold
or it won't.

When there's about a hundred feet of line left in the
tub, I go to pick up the keg. And that's when a loop of
line snags in the tub. Without thinking about it I reach
my hand out to clear the snag.

Big mistake.

Snag whips around my wrist, fast as the blink of an
eye. There's no time to get loose of it. There's no time
even to take a deep breath or get ready for what happens next. Because the moment the snag closes

around my wrist, the line jerks me over the side and the next thing I know I'm flying out of the boat and into the water.

Into the cold water and down. Pulled down by the fish that hooked me. By the fish that's trying to kill me.

22

Keg Rider

IT happens so fast, I don't have time to take a deep breath. One second I'm in the boat, the next I'm underwater. Water so cold, it makes my bones ache, but I don't care about that. All I care about is getting the line off my wrist and kicking back up to where there's air. Air is all that matters.

Cold water makes my eyes sting bad, but I can see what I got to do, sort of. See the loop of line snagged on my wrist. Probably cutting into my skin, but I can't feel it. Can't feel nothing but the panic exploding in my lungs and the cold, stabbing pain in my throat. A fish must feel like this, getting yanked from the nice safe water into the air, where it can't breathe.

Get loose. No room in my head for anything but "get loose."

I'm scratching at my wrist, prying under the loop of line, but it's way too tight.

Think. You got to think how to get loose.

I follow the line out with my other hand and try pulling on it, maybe get enough slack to slip it off, but the line slips through my fingers and I can't get a grip.

Hands weak, getting weaker.

No time. No time!

I'm kicking, trying to get back to the surface, fighting the steady tug on the line.

Air! Must have air!

The surface is shimmering above me. Looks like a silver mirror made of liquid. Beautiful. Air bubbles coming out of my mouth rise up and melt into the shimmering silver mirror. Never seen nothing so pretty.

MUST HAVE AIR!

Who's making all the noise? Shouting while you're underwater? That's really stupid. Can't shout underwater, you fool.

Relax. Quit fighting. Open your mouth and inhale. You know you want to. You have to inhale something, right? Maybe your lungs can take air out of the water like a fish. Mom always said you were part fish, right? So breathe underwater and prove it.

I open my mouth and try to inhale but nothing comes in. I can't get my throat unstuck; it's like there's a ring of ice around my neck.

SKIFF BEAMAN, DON'T YOU DARE BREATHE WATER!

Can't help it, Mom. Got to breathe something. Got to. Got to. Got to.

Don't give up! Listen to me! Rule Number Three! Never give up! The surface is right above your head! Kick! Kick! Kick!

Too far away. Can't make it. So tired.

Try, Skiffy, try!

I kick and kick until there's nothing left in my legs. I want to laugh because it's so funny, getting drowned by a fish. Funniest thing in the world. But my throat is closed and the ice has gone into my lungs and laughing hurts too much. Good joke, though. Really, really funny.

Rule Number Three: Never give up. Don't ever give up!

Blackness shimmers down fro... the warm dark.

Time to sleep.

Coughing hurts so bad, it wakes me up. Is this drowning? Water in my mouth, making me choke, but there's air, too. Real air. I'm at the surface, bobbing up and down. Voice in my head made me wake up, but I can't remember what it said or how I got here.

Choking and coughing hurts worse than drowning. Plus I can't see because my eyes are drenched in salt water.

KLANG!

Back of my head whacks into something hollow. Turn around, flailing my arms, find the keg bobbing next to me. Grab hold. Pull myself up, so my shoulders are clear of the water. Hug that keg with all my might while I get my wind back.

What happened? Can't put it straight in my head. Okay. Hand tangled in the line, I remember that. Getting yanked into the water. Tried to get loose and couldn't. Thought about inhaling water but couldn't do that, either.

So why am I alive?

When my eyes finally clear up, I see why. There it is, circling inside the wall of white fog. The giant bluefin back on the surface, swimming in a big circle around me and the keg.

Does it know it almost killed me and then saved my life?

I want to shout out to the fish, ask it where my boat is, but my throat hurts too much.

Figure my little skiff can't be too far away. Somewhere inside the wall of fog. Got to find that boat before too long or the cold water will kill me. Already I'm so numb, I can't hardly feel a thing from the neck down.

Cold water is sucking the heat out of me. And they say if your blood gets too cold, you die.

Hang around the town wharf, you hear about it all the time. How falling out of a boat can kill a man if he stays in cold water for long. They say in the wintertime, with water close to freezing, you ain't got but ten or fifteen minutes before your heart quits beating. Summer water takes longer. Figure maybe an hour or two.

Part of me wants to let go of the keg and swim around looking for the skiff before I'm too weak to move my arms. But the keg is helping me float, letting me get my strength back, and if I let go I may never find it again. Then where'd I be?

If I was wearing my life jacket it might be different. Keeping hold of the keg wouldn't be so important. But like a darn fool I left my life jacket in the bottom of the boat, under the seat. Life jacket don't do much good if you don't wear it. My dad must have told me that a thousand times, but I guess it didn't take.

Too late to worry about that now. Mistake's already been made. Worry about keeping your head above water. Worry about holding on to the keg. Worry about finding the skiff. Can't be far, can it? No wind to speak of. Nothing to move it but the tide and current, and that same tide and current is moving me and the keg in the same direction.

Can't be far. Look around, maybe you'll see it. The fog may lift again. See that little boat, you swim for it with all your might. Meantime, ride the keg and hope for the best.

Shivering cold reminds me of the day Mom died.

She'd been real sick for a long time, and we all knew what was coming, so I should have been ready, but it don't work like that. Knowing a thing is bound to happen don't make it easier. Thing is, you keep hoping for a miracle right up to the end and then when it don't it's like the floor disappears and you're falling but you never hit bottom.

When it happened, all I could think to do was run. First I ran in circles around her room. Then I ran around the house kicking at the stupid snow. Then I ran across the road and into the woods and climbed up a tree and lay there hugging the icy branch while the ambulance came and went. I watched Captain Keelson and his wife drive up and go inside and then Dad came out with them and Captain Keelson shouted my name and asked me to come home, please, and be with my father, but I kept hugging the branch and hoping I'd wake up from a bad dream and Mom would be okay except I knew it wasn't a dream and I'd never ever see her again or hear her voice, ever ever ever, and that's when she said, *Skiffy, go to your father,* her voice in my head as clear as day, and I knew that's what she'd want me to do and I did it, I came down from the tree and went back to the house and told Dad not to worry, everything would be okay because Mom said so, and he give me a look so sad, it hurt to breathe and then he went and lay down on the TV couch and didn't say nothing for a long time.

I guess Dad can't hear Mom's voice like I can, or if he does he won't listen.

Anyhow, I'm riding that keg and thinking about my mom and my dad and home and the *Mary Rose* and that's when the skiff comes out of the fog, bobbing up and down like it's trying to say "hello."

First I think my eyes are fooling, but there it is, big as life, looking like it missed me.

I keep hold of the keg for a minute in case the skiff decides to disappear again. Maybe it's a trick to make me let go of the keg. But the skiff keeps drifting closer and closer and when I can almost reach out and touch it I let go the keg and kick like mad and pull myself into the boat.

Then I lie in the bottom of the skiff and laugh like a maniac because it feels so good to be alive.

23

A Nantucket Sleigh Ride

IT ain't the cold makes me shiver. The summer air will warm me up soon enough. What gets me shaking is how scared I was the whole time in the water.

Down the town wharf they tell spooky stories about fishermen who fall from boats, but I always figured it was like ghost talk around a campfire. I guess those kind of things are make-believe until they happen to you, and then it don't seem so far-fetched. Turns out falling from a boat is dead easy — any fool can do it.

When the shivering eases, I sit up and look around. Fog. Seems like it just won't leave me alone.

I find my soggy life jacket and put it on. Just in case.

And that reminds me of the fish. How it was circling when I grabbed hold of the keg. But the water is gray and glassy and calm. No big bluefin up on the surface, that's for sure. And the keg is still bobbing next to the skiff. Which means the fish must have got free somehow. Pulled the barb or cut the line. Only fair, I suppose. Fish had a chance to drown me and didn't.

I tell myself it's okay. Tell myself not to feel too bad. Easy to want a fish more than anything in the world until you almost been drowned. That sure changes the way you look at things. Still, I do look around for the harpoon. Never know when another big fish might decide to come by.

But the harpoon is gone. Must have gone over when I did.

Face it, boy. You'll have to catch a giant tuna some other day. You're wet and shivering and hungry again. Out of bait, out of luck. Time to pack up and go home. So I reach over the side, lift the keg into the skiff, shove it under the front seat, and start to pull in the line. Coiling it neat in the tub. Thinking how harmless it looks until it's wrapped around your wrist and you're being dragged under.

Next thing, I yank my hand away from the line like I been shocked with electricity. *Because the line feels alive.*

The fish is still on! Must be right under the boat. Resting up from all the hard work it's done trying to drag me under. Only now it's feeling much better, thank you. Because the line is running back out of the tub. Running fast. And this time I know enough to keep my hands away. I aim to give it room. Don't even want to touch the keg; that's what got me in trouble the last time, trying to throw it over. Figure the keg will pop out from under the seat when all the line runs out.

But it don't pop out. Tension on the line locks the keg under the front seat and then the skiff jerks out from under my feet. I land hard on the rear seat. The skiff is moving. Line is twanging like the high string on a steel guitar as the fish rises up to the surface, pulling the skiff behind it. Seems crazy, but the tuna weighs more than the skiff and me combined, and even with a harpoon barb buried in its back it has the strength to run.

Nothing I can do but hang on. My dad says in the old days men going after whales in small boats sometimes got what they call a Nantucket sleigh ride. Dragged behind a whale trying as hard as it can to get away from the human beings that hunted it. Them Nantucket whalers thought it was more fun than Disneyland, getting a fast ride from a whale. Not me, though. I wish it would stop. What if the skiff tips over? What if I get thrown out and the skiff disappears into the fog again? I got my life jacket on, but so what? Cold'll kill me for sure this time.

The skiff skates along, throwing up a wake. Kind of creeps me out to be going this fast without a motor. A bluefin tuna ain't a whale, but still it's way bigger than me, and a million times stronger, pound for pound. I'm thinking get the knife and cut the line, but something in me says no. Never give up, even when it scares you half to death. Especially then. So I hang on with both hands and pray everything will be okay. Dear Lord, don't let it sink me. And don't let the barb pull loose. And don't let the line break.

I figure God got more important things to do than

help a boy catch a fish, but you never know. Never hurts to ask, my mom used to say.

No idea how long the sleigh ride lasts. Could be ten minutes, could be an hour. But there comes a time when the line stops pulling and the skiff slows down and stops. I look around for the fish and there it is, fifty or sixty feet away. Rolling around on the surface like it don't know which side is up. That big fin all wobbly and weak, and blood coming from the place where the barb went in, and the shiny dark eye staring at me, as if to say, *look what you did.*

I caught lots of small fish, mackerel and pollock and cod and flounder, and cleaned 'em, too. Never bothered me, once I got used to it. But this is different. This time I feel sorry for the fish. Could have drowned me but it didn't and now it's dying and I'm the one who killed it. Big beautiful creature so alive, it seemed like it could never die. But I know better. I knew it when I threw the harpoon.

Then I get to thinking what it will mean if I can get the fish to shore and sell it to Mr. Nagahachi. New engine for the *Mary Rose*. New traps to replace those that were cut. Something nice for my dad, that will make him feel like he used to feel before things went bad. The look on Tyler's face when he sees me bring in a really big fish. New bike, new life, new everything.

When the fish stops moving I get out the oars and work the skiff as close as I can. Ready to back off if it comes alive. But the fight has gone out of the fish. The gills are barely moving and the bright blue color is getting dull.

I know from what my dad said that I need to get a rope around the tail. Control the tail and you control the fish. But how do I do that without jumping into the water? Because I ain't going back in the water, no matter what.

Fish rolls over and looks at me. That big dark eye starting to cloud over. Weight of the head starting to pull it down.

Now or never, boy.

My hands are shaking, but not so bad I can't tie a loop in a rope. I work the rope into the water and around the half-moon curve of the tail and I'm thinking, this ain't so hard, what was I afraid of, when the fish decides it's not quite ready to die.

Tail slaps the water, spraying me. The loop tightens

and now I got my hands full, hanging on as the tail lashes back and forth. I brace my feet against the seat and cling to the rope.

Once at the Fourth of July picnic they had tug-of-war, and the losing side got pulled into a puddle, which looked pretty funny unless it was you in the mud. Mom said the secret was to know when to let go, to make the other side fall first. But as scared as I am to hold on, I'm even more scared to let go. Give the fish an inch and it'll get its tail under the water and then there will be no stopping it. I been there and I don't want to go back. So I hang on as it thrashes around. Hang on until it feels like my arms will get pulled from the sockets. Hang on with my heart beating so hard, it makes my face hot.

Finally the thrashing slows and then the big fish shivers and stops moving. It's still alive but not strong enough to fight, or to keep me from looping the rope around the stern cleats.

When I got the rope hitched I take a breather and decide what to do next. All the thinking I done about harpooning a big fish, I never thought about what happens after. Too big to haul into the boat, even if I was strong enough, which I'm not.

Only thing I can think to do is drag the fish behind the skiff, tail first.

My arms are so weak, I can barely pull on the starter rope, but the old outboard fires right up anyhow. I put it in gear and steer until the compass finds west. I can feel the weight of the fish behind the skiff. Outboard chugging as if to say, what's going on? What did you do? How'd the skiff get so heavy all of a sudden?

Caught me a giant tuna, yes I did.

Proud of yourself, are you?

Matter of fact, yes. Tired and cold and hungry, but mighty proud, too.

Keep steering, fool. Don't let it fall off to the south. Steer west. True west. That's where the land is. That's where the ocean ends. Hold the course, boy. Thirty miles to home. Thirty miles to find Mr. Nagahachi. Thirty miles to sell the fish and then everything will be good again.

Everything will be perfect.

24

The Angel in the Mist

LITTLE flat-bottomed skiff like mine was never meant to tow anything heavy. With a giant fish behind, it starts to wallow. That means the back end of the skiff gets low in the water as the outboard tries to push it forward, then it comes up hard against the rope and slows down. When that happens the outboard makes a funny sound, like an old cat trying to cough up a fur ball. Don't sound good, that's for sure, and it makes me worry about a wave coming over the stern.

I try to balance the skiff by shifting gear to the front

and scrunching myself forward, but it don't help much. Doubt we're going more than five miles an hour, me and the big fish. So if the tide is going out — and I think it is — we're not making much headway at all. A mile or two each hour.

Not near enough.

Come on, little skiff, I'm thinking. You're a good boat. You can do it. Keep heading west. Head for Spinney Cove. Head for home. Get this mighty fish to the dock before Mr. Nagahachi goes home for the day. Before my dad figures out that me and the skiff and the last harpoon are missing.

Do the math, though, and it don't sound good. At this rate it'll take fifteen hours to get back to shore. Tuna won't keep for fifteen hours, even in cold water. Have to sell it for cat food, a few pennies on the pound.

Then I remember that the tide turns every six hours. So pretty soon it'll be coming from behind, pushing the skiff toward shore. Or the fog might lift and I can make a deal with one of the tuna boats out on the fishing grounds. Give 'em part of the profit to tow me and the big fish back to the dock. Hate to split up the money, but if it means a higher price for a fresh fish, it'd be worth it, right?

I'm still calculating the profit when the outboard starts to sputter.

"Hey motor? Please don't you quit on me now. Take me home, I'll give you a new carburetor. I'll have you rebuilt good as new."

But it ain't the outboard. I know better. It's the gas. Been running for two or three hours and now it's down to fumes. I give the fuel tank a shake and the motor picks up for a time, but then it sort of fades away, *oop-oop-oop,* and makes a little clunk, and that's it, no more outboard motor.

Quiet all of a sudden. Hush of the fog. Whisper of water on the hull. Little thump as the swell pushes the big fish up against the back of the skiff. Tail thumping soft as a puppy's tail to remind me of what I done. Only other noise is me getting out the oars.

All along I knew it would come to this. Even without towing a lot of extra weight the skiff wouldn't hold enough gas for the whole round trip. So it was always going to come down to me rowing the last few miles. Except this is more than a few miles. More like twenty miles.

I done a fair bit of rowing, up the creek and back, and around the harbor, but nothing like twenty miles in one shot.

Figure each mile could be worth as much as a thousand dollars, if I can get the fish to the dock before it goes bad. Thousand bucks a mile! That makes me put my back into it. But from the very first pull I know how hard it's going to be. I can feel the huge weight of the fish fighting the oars. Plus it's hard to watch the compass and keep to the right course when you're facing backward and pulling with all your might.

What choice do I have? No choice at all. I got myself into this mess and now I got to row myself out of it, plain and simple. I heard stories of men rowed a hundred miles when they had to, in worse weather than this, and without food or water.

Which reminds me I'm out of food and water, too. Wish I hadn't chomped down that last sandwich. I sure could use it now! My stomach feels so empty, it hurts. Scrambled eggs and sausage and toast with raspberry jam, that's what my stomach wants. Then a warm bed and a soft pillow. Or curl up next to Dad on the TV couch and forget about everything wet and cold.

"Hey Big Bluefin," I say. "Give us a push, why don't you?"

Big Bluefin ain't talking. Every now and then the giant tail makes a feeble slap, but the strength is fading and pretty soon that tail will stop moving forever. The great head lolls around and looks at me as it rises on a swell. Big sad eyes that say good-bye.

I pull hard on the oars, and then the rope comes up tight and the whole skiff jerks to a stop.

Got to find the rhythm or I'll never get anywhere. Pull, ease. Pull, ease. Pull. Pull. Pull. Time it so the rope never goes slack. And don't forget to check the compass. Without a compass you'll row in circles, sure as Christmas, because one arm is always stronger. Same as a hunter lost in the woods will walk in circles, if he don't have a star to guide him, or know that moss mostly grows on the north side of trees.

Fog this bad, no way to know exactly where land is until I hit the shore. So stop thinking about home and the harbor and the creek you know like the back of your hand. Stop thinking about how hungry and thirsty you are. Don't think about nothing but rowing.

Don't think about how much it hurts.

Don't think about the blisters on your hands.

Don't think at all.

Pull.

Ease.

Pull.

Pull.

Pull.

I'm like a machine. A tired and worn-out machine that can't stop or it'll fall apart. Can't hardly tell where my arms end and the oars begin.

Pull.

Pull.

Pull.

Don't think.

Pull.

Pull.

Pull.

Hours go by. Or it could be days and weeks and

months and years, for all I know, because time gets strange when every part of you is tired and hurting.

I remember sitting at my desk in school, last period of the last class of the last day, and waiting for the minute hand to tick along until the bell rang. The last ten minutes of that class took a week at least. This is worse, much worse. As if each minute is an hour and an hour is forever.

All that's left of me is the rowing part and the hurting part. The thinking part of me is hiding in the back of my head and won't come out. Why should it? Nothing out here but hungry and hurting and thirsty and miserable.

Pull.

Pull.

Pull.

The glow in the fog fades to a dull gray. Takes me a year or two to realize the sun is going down. That's how long I been rowing. And every lick of it feels like I been rowing in place, never getting anywhere. Rowing against the tide, against the weight. Moving around the same patch of black water, towing a giant fish. Like walking up a steep hill with heavy iron boots, only you can never get to the top of the hill because it keeps getting higher and higher and the boots get heavier and heavier.

Pull.

Pull.

Pull.

I want to tell the fish it won. It beat me. For every stroke of the oars it pulled back harder. It never gave up. It tuckered me out. It drowned me in fog and dark.

Pull.

Pull.

Pull.

The fog turns from day fog to night fog. It must be getting cooler, but I can't feel it. My hands been numb for a long time, but when night comes they feel warm, which don't seem right, and then my hands slip off the oars and I fall off the seat and land in the bottom of the skiff.

Put my hands to my face and realize my hands are bleeding and that's what made 'em slip away from the oars. I get back into the seat and take a deep breath and try to clear my head, which ain't easy. I stopped being hungry a long time ago, but not eating makes it hard to think.

What can I do? Comes to me there's only two possibilities. Cut the fish loose, or find a way to keep rowing.

Cut the fish loose is giving up, and that means breaking Rule Number Three. But Rule Number One is think smart. Maybe thinking smart is cutting loose the fish. Which is more important, never giving up or thinking smart?

I'm trying to decide when I notice something under my foot. A lumpy sandwich bag. Which don't make no sense, since I ate all my sandwiches a long time ago.

Or did I?

Takes all my strength to reach down and pick up the plastic bag with my bloody fingers and hold it up so I can see it. I'll be darn. A plain old peanut butter and jelly sandwich.

Bar of solid gold couldn't look any finer.

My hands are so slippery and shaky, I have to tear the bag open with my teeth. Sandwich! Squished and soggy don't matter when you're starving. I eat the whole thing in one fat, wonderful bite. It tastes sticky and sweet. Better than candy. Better than anything.

That little bit of food clears my head and stops me shaking. It helps me decide what to do. Helps me think how to be smart and never give up, both at the same time.

What happens is I remember a true story Mr. Woodwell told me once, that happened long ago. In the old days they fished from schooners, big wooden ships with white canvas sails that took the fishermen far offshore to the Grand Banks fishing grounds. Each schooner carried a bunch of wooden dories stacked on deck, and when they got to the fishing grounds the men got into the dories and rowed away, looking for cod and haddock.

This one guy got lost in a winter storm and couldn't find the schooner. He's a hundred miles at sea and can't find his ship. All his gear is washed away, except for his oars. He knows his hands will soon get frost-bite and then he won't be able to grip the oars. Before that happens he dips his hands in the cold water and freezes them to the oar handles so he can't let go. And he rows all the way from the Grand Banks, off Nova

Scotia, to Gloucester, Massachusetts. Lost his hands to the frostbite but rowed all the way home and lived to tell the tale.

He never gave up. He did what he had to do.

What I got to do is somehow keep my hands from slipping off the oars. So I cut two pieces of rope. Lash my left hand to the left oar and tie the rope with a good knot.

There. Can't let go.

Lashing my right hand is much harder, so hard it brings tears to my eyes, but I finally manage to pull the knot tight with my teeth. Both hands tied to the oars. Can't let go, can't give up.

Ready?

Ready.

Pull.

Pull.

Pull.

One day near the end when my mom was really sick she called me into her room. Her voice was so small and quiet, I had to lean close and smell the sick on her breath. I didn't care. I wanted to be that close. I wanted to feel her fingers feather-light on my cheek.

I know you're still a small boy, Skiff Beaman, but I've got a big job for you.

Anything, Mom. Anything at all.

I want you to take care of your father. You understand?

Sure, Mom. Take care of Dad.

Swear on a stack of pancakes?

I swear, Mom.

Thing is, I'd have done that anyhow, without her asking. Mom knew that, but she wanted to hear me say it, to put her easy in her mind.

Comes to me that the only really good reason to keep on rowing is to keep that promise. And if I cut the fish loose I can get home sooner. Makes sense. Only thing, I can't cut the rope because my hands are lashed to the oars. So there it is.

Pull.

Pull.

Pull.

One time we all went out for a picnic on the *Mary*

Rose. Anchored behind Boone Island, out of the wind, and Mom put a checkered tablecloth over the engine cover and passed out fried chicken on paper plates and potato salad and pickles and stuff, and home-made blueberry pie for dessert. I ate so much, I like to bust and started complaining about a full stomach and too much food, and she said never complain about too much food, that's an insult to the cook and an insult to all the hungry people in the world.

I sassed her and had to stay down in the cabin for the rest of the picnic. When we got back to the dock, Mom came down in the cabin and said have you got over being a smart mouth? and I said no. Mom shook her head and sat down on the bunk and said what am I going to do with you? Don't care what you do, I told her, my stomach hurts and you don't care. Mom said look me in the eye and say that and I looked her in the eye and I couldn't say it because it wasn't true. She smiled then and said, you have as much stubborn in you as a full-grown man. I hope someday you put it to good use.

That was our last picnic on the *Mary Rose*.

Pull.

Pull.

Pull.

When Mom got sick I kept wishing I had a time machine so I could go back and fix things. Take back all the mean words I ever said to her. Change what made her sick. Change myself into a better person that didn't ruin picnics.

Pull.

Pull.

Pull.

Can't feel my arms. Can't feel my hands. All I can feel is the weight of the skiff and the big fish and the fog pressing down. Brain ain't working right. Something wrong but I don't know what. Almost like I'm asleep but I can't be asleep because I'm still rowing. My eyes are wide open but the compass has gone blurry. Am I still headed for shore?

Pull.

Pull.

Pull.

Can't stop. Want to give up but can't. Now I'm watching me pull on the oars. Like I'm floating just above, watching Skiff Beaman row and row and row.

Crazy boy, where's he think he's going? Going to Boone Island for a picnic. Going to get it right this time.

Pull.

Pull.

Pull.

Can't see the compass, can't see the fish, can't see the end of my oars dipping into the water. Only thing I can see is the funny-looking giant striding high above the fog. Tall thing with skinny legs and a bright white halo shining behind its head. Do giants have halos? Can't be a giant. Giants don't exist, do they? Must be an angel. An angel in the mist with eyes like beams of light.

Don't matter. Must keep rowing.

Then the angel comes out of the fog and it's a boat not an angel and the halo is a spotlight shining down from the tuna tower and a man shouts from the tower but I can't understand what he's saying and it might be a dream tempting me to give up so I don't stop rowing, I never stop rowing until my father jumps down from *Fin Chaser* and picks me up, oars and all, and carries me to sleep.

25

The Tail on the Door

SMALL BOY HARPOONS BIGGEST FISH

Portland Press Herald—The largest bluefin tuna taken by harpoon in Maine waters this season was caught by twelve-year-old Samuel "Skiff" Beaman, Jr., of Spinney Cove. The 900-pound fish fetched a record price but very nearly cost young Mr. Beaman his life. After harpooning the trophy tuna and securing it to his ten-foot skiff, Beaman ran out of fuel and rowed from Jeffrey's Ledge to within five miles of shore, a distance of twenty-five miles, in unusually heavy fog.

The Coast Guard cutter *Reliance* and a number of commercial fishing vessels had been searching through the night for the young harpooner when he was found by his father, Samuel Beaman, Sr., aboard *Fin Chaser,* a private tuna boat owned by Jack Croft of Spinney Cove. Mr. Croft reports that the boy was badly dehydrated by the time he was discovered, and that he had apparently been rowing without pause for more than twelve hours.

The boy was treated at the Maine Medical Center in Portland and released the next day. He is expected to make a full recovery.

The newspaper article is in my scrapbook now, along with a photocopy of the check from Mr. Nagahachi. Too bad they didn't take a picture of the fish, but everybody was so worried about me, I guess they forgot. Dad says not to fret, there will be other fish and we can take a picture then. Have to wait until next year, at least, what with getting the *Mary Rose* fixed and school starting and things to do around the house.

Today Dad vacuumed the living room, which is a first. We're cleaning up because Mr. Woodwell has been invited to supper and Dad says it don't matter if the old man is halfway blind, he still knows dirt from dirt. Plus he's an honored guest and I'm lucky he didn't have me arrested for stealing the harpoon.

The deal is, Dad is going to show me how to make a new harpoon for Mr. Woodwell, to replace the one I lost. Also I'm supposed to help the old geezer around the shed for nothing, for as long as he needs me. Like I mind, right? When the truth is I'd rather be in that boat shed than almost anywhere else in the world. Except out in a boat, of course.

The other good thing, besides fixing the *Mary Rose,* is that Dad is going to meetings to help him stay sober. Says he has to take it one day at a time. Says that looking for me in the fog scared the beer right out of him. We'll see. So far, so good.

As for Tyler, the lying weasel, he swore up and down he didn't cut my traps, but his father didn't believe him, so he lost the use of the Boston Whaler for a year. Big deal. Dad says Jack Croft doesn't know what to do with the boy and probably wishes he had me for a son, but somehow I doubt that. Blood is blood, and you got to keep together with your family, even if they mess up. Friends, too. Like Dad says, he found two things in the fog, me and his old pal Jack, who didn't think nothing of risking his boat for a true friend.

Which brings me to the biggest fish. The fish that almost drowned me and then saved me and then took me for a ride, and then nearly killed me all over again. The biggest fish in the big blue sea got flown to the other side of the world and was served up at weddings and ceremonies and birthday parties all over Japan, where they call the giant bluefin tuna *hon maguro* and believe that it melts in your mouth and into your soul.

All except the tail. The tail I nailed up above the outhouse door, where everybody can see it. Dad offered to tear down the old outhouse so nobody would think to sing that stupid song again, but I said leave her be.

I like things just the way they are.

AFTeR WORDS™

RODMAN PHILBRICK'S
The Young Man and the Sea

CONTENTS

About the Author
Q&A with Rodman Philbrick
Rod's Writing Tips
A Sneak Peek at *Freak the Mighty*

After Words™ guide by Anamika Bhatnagar

About the Author

After years of writing mysteries and suspense thrillers for adults, Rodman Philbrick decided to try his hand at a novel for young readers. That novel, *Freak the Mighty*, was published in 1993 to great acclaim and stellar reviews. In addition to being named an ALA Best Book for Young Adults and winning several state awards, it was also made into the Miramax feature film *The Mighty* in 1998. Rod returns to Maxwell Kane's story in a sequel, *Max the Mighty*, a fast-paced cross-country odyssey.

Rod takes young readers to the American West in his exhilarating tale of two brothers on the run in *The Fire Pony*, winner of the Capital Choice Award, and on to a land where nothing is as it seems in the science-fiction adventure *REM World*. His thought-provoking novel *The Last Book in the Universe*, also an ALA Best Book for Young Adults, takes place in a futuristic world where no one reads anymore. Rod thought back to his New England roots and knowledge of boat building to write *The Young Man and the Sea*. *School Library Journal* praised its "wide-open adventure" and "heart-pounding suspense" and named it a Best Book of the Year in 2004.

Rodman Philbrick has also written several spine-tingling series for young readers with his wife, Lynn Harnett, including The House on Cherry Street and The Werewolf Chronicles. Rod and Lynn divide their time between homes on the coast of Maine and in the Florida Keys.

Q&A with Rodman Philbrick

Q: *You started writing when you were in the sixth grade. Did you always want to be a writer? Do you remember any of your first stories?*

A: I always wanted to be a writer, although at various times I also wanted to be an astronaut, a doctor, a lawyer, and so on. The first short story I remember completing was a five-page, trick-ending thing called "The President's Barber." Each day the White House barber gives the president a shave with a straight razor, and each day he secretly decides whether or not he'll let the president live, or cut his throat.

Q: *Have you always written for kids?*

A: No. For the first fifteen years of my career as a novelist, I wrote only for adult readers — mysteries, suspense novels, thrillers, and so on. Then I stumbled on the idea for a story that had been happening in my backyard, so to speak, and wrote *Freak the Mighty* in the summer of 1992. Since then I've published books for young readers as well as novels intended for adults.

Q: *Did you have a hard time getting your first book published? What other jobs did you have when you were first starting out as a writer?*

A: I had a lot of trouble getting published. I wrote my first novel at sixteen and then wrote eight more before I finally found a publisher at age twenty-eight. During those years, I worked as a longshoreman, a carpenter, a roofer, and a boat-builder.

Q: *Is* Freak the Mighty *based on a true story?*
A: The idea for *Freak the Mighty* was inspired by the personality of a real boy. Like Kevin, one of the book's two main characters, he suffered from a disease that made him very short. Like Kevin, he had a big friend who sometimes carried him around. And, like Kevin, the real boy was highly intelligent and interested in both language and science. His mother, like the Fair Gwen, was and is quite beautiful. There the similarity ends — the plot of the story is pure fiction.

Q: *Max, the other main character, is also unusual. What inspired you to create him?*
A: I'd seen my little friend riding around on the shoulders of one of his big buddies. I didn't know the big guy, so that allowed me to invent an entirely fictional character. I thought it would be interesting if he had some darkness in his past — a father in jail, his mother dead.

Q: *You've said that* Freak the Mighty *is about a writer learning to find his voice, and that theme recurs in your novel* The Last Book in the Universe. *How did you find your voice?*
A: Over many years and over many thousands of pages. Learning to write a readable, compelling story was hard work for me.

Q: *What inspired you to write* The Last Book in the Universe?

A: The editor Michael Cart asked me to contribute a story to an anthology called *Tomorrowland*. At first, all I came up with was an intriguing title, "The Last Book in the Universe." Then I had to think up a world where there might be a "last book," and think about why people had stopped reading. After finishing the short story, which was eventually published, I couldn't stop thinking about the world the narrator, Spaz, lived in and I set about making it a full-scale novel. No doubt many of the "sci-fi" elements came from my love of movies like the original *The Time Machine*, and from my adolescent fascination with comic book adventures.

Q: *Did the short story change a lot when you expanded it into a novel?*

A: The short story is pretty much confined to Spaz and his mentor, Ryter. To make it an interesting novel, I needed more characters and more adventure. So I invented Eden and populated it with people who had "improved" themselves genetically. Then I added Spaz's sister, Bean, put her in peril, and the adventure began.

Q: *You've written books that are based in a familiar setting, like* Freak the Mighty *and this one, and others that take place in lands you've invented, like* REM World *and* The Last Book in the Universe. *Which is easier to write about?*

A: Imagined worlds are always a bit more difficult for me. I can't write about a place until it seems real in my own head, so that obviously takes a leap of imagination that's not required for the real world.

Q: *The characters in your books have such interesting, evocative names: Gram and Grim, Loretta Lee, and Killer Kane from* Freak the Mighty; *Spaz from* The Last Book in the Universe; *and Skiff Beaman from* The Young Man and the Sea. *How do you come up with them?*

A: Names are important to me. I can never really get started on a story until the characters have names that mean something to me. Sometimes the names come out of thin air, other times from newspaper articles or songs.

Q: *You've written several books with your wife, Lynn Harnett. Is it hard to write a book with someone else?*

A: It depends on who you're writing with! Lynn has been my only collaborator, and she is an experienced writer and an editor. When my publisher asked if we'd like to write a series of scary stories for young readers, we said yes. Our first series was a haunted house trilogy called The House on Cherry Street. So far, we've written ten books together, but we continue to write books on our own as well.

Q: *What inspired you to write* The Young Man and the Sea?

A: The notion of a boy harpooning a giant bluefin tuna came to me when my younger brother, Jonathan (a teenager at the time), worked as a crewman on a tuna boat. He told me tales of the giant fish and it always stuck in my mind.

Q: *The title of the book brings to mind Ernest Hemingway's 1952 novella* The Old Man and the Sea. *Are the similarities in the title intentional?*

A: Before I had a definite title, my editor and I called this "the young man and the sea book" because I had mentioned that Hemingway's famous story about an old man and the sea had inspired the part of my story that involves going after a big fish in a small boat. My original title for the book was "Lobster Boy," but people kept expecting a kid with claws for hands, sort of the "lobster version" of *Edward Scissorhands*. Finally we decided that *The Young Man and the Sea* worked best as a title because it openly acknowledges Hemingway's influence. Oddly enough, the British edition of the book reverted to the old title, *Lobster Boy*.

Q: *Is the character of Skiff Beaman based on a real person? What about Mr. Woodwell?*

A: Parts of Skiff's personality were drawn from people I knew as a kid. There actually was a Mr. Woodwell. When I knew him he was an elderly gentleman, a retired schoolteacher who was rebuilding an old Friendship sloop. As a young man I sailed Down East with him. We were headed for the race at Friendship, Maine, but got fogged in in Casco Bay. I combined Mr. Woodwell's wise and gentle nature with that of another, highly skilled boatbuilder who lived up the river from me, a man who had a boat shed very much like the one in the book.

Q: *Skiff has a very distinctive voice. Do people from Maine really talk like that?*

A: To my ear, many do. Skiff's way of talking is somewhat modified — the real residents of "Spinney Cove" tend to drop the letter *r* even more.

Q: *There is a great deal of detailed information about trapping lobsters and boatbuilding. Did you have to do a lot of research to write about those subjects?*

A: Before I was a published author, I was a boatbuilder for a number of years, and therefore I know quite a lot about boats and boat repair. For information about traps and lobster fishing, I consulted my friend Paul Brown, a lobsterman in Kittery, Maine.

Q: *When you travel on your boat, what's your favorite destination?*

A: I have two favorite destinations, one north and one south. When we're in Maine my favorite destination is the Isles of Shoals, a group of islands seven miles offshore. When we're in the Florida Keys, my wife, Lynn, and I sometimes take a twenty-eight-mile run across Florida Bay and explore the wind-swept beaches at Cape Sable, which is part of the Everglades.

Q: *Do you enjoy fishing?*

A: I'm an avid fisherman, and I practice the fine art of angling as frequently as possible. In Maine I fish mostly for striped bass and bluefish. In the Florida Keys I fish for a variety of species, including the giant tarpon. Except when I'm going to cook fish for supper, I always practice "hook and release."

Q: *Are you working on a new book right now? What can you tell us about it?*

A: I'm always working on a book. That's what I do — besides fishing, I mean. At the moment, I'm writing a novel with the working title "The True Adventures of Homer Figg." It's about a boy from Maine who runs away from home and follows his older brother into battle during the Civil War.

Rod's Writing Tips

Rodman Philbrick began writing when he was in the sixth grade. At first, he kept his stories a secret because writing didn't seem "cool" or "normal," but when he turned sixteen, he decided to send his first novel — about a boy who admires his best friend, a genius who eventually dies tragically — to several publishers. Although the novel was rejected, Rod didn't give up. When he was twenty-eight, his career as a writer took off with the publication of a suspense novel for adults. Here, Rod shares some of his tips for writers of all ages.

1. Getting started is easier than you think. You can begin by telling a story to yourself — one that you don't have to share with anyone else — either by writing in a journal or typing at your computer.

2. Even when you're writing fiction, you have to tell the truth. This doesn't mean you have to write about real people or even your own life, but you can make your readers believe in the characters you're creating if their emotions are clear. Joy makes you feel capable of flight. Anger puts murder in your heart. An insult physically hurts. These are feelings we can all relate to.

3. A good memory helps. Again, even if you're not writing about your own past or present experiences, the characters and situations you're writing about need to feel real. Think about your bedroom. Where do you sit when you're in there? What can you see from the windows? What does it smell like outside? These concrete details can help you

shape a world that your readers will recognize — even if you're writing about life on another planet.

4. Play the "what if" game. Ask yourself a question, and find out where the answer leads you. You could start with a question about your own life: What if you found out you had a twin brother or sister that no one had told you about? What if you wanted to meet your twin, but your parents said it wasn't a good idea? What would you do? Or perhaps you could start with a question about the world in general: What if kids never had to go to school? What if they never learned to read or write? What would they do instead? What would their lives be like?

5. Listen to the voices in your head. Sometimes when you're thinking about nothing in particular, a word or phrase or even a full sentence enters your brain. One day, I was on a long drive from New York to Maine when I heard a voice say, "I never had a brain until Freak came along and let me borrow his for a while, and that's the truth, the whole truth." Maybe you're just daydreaming, or maybe it's the beginning of your next story.

Rodman Philbrick,
Age 17

A Sneak Peek at *Freak the Mighty*

Rodman Philbrick's first novel for young readers, *Freak the Mighty*, was published in 1993 to rave reviews. It has since sold more than one million copies in the United States alone, and it has been published in German, Chinese, and Italian, among other languages. Here's a special preview of the intriguing first chapter.

I never had a brain until Freak came along and let me borrow his for a while, and that's the truth, the whole truth. The unvanquished truth, is how Freak would say it, and for a long time it was him who did the talking. Except I had a way of saying things with my fists and my feet even before we became Freak the Mighty, slaying dragons and fools and walking high above the world.

Called me Kicker for a time — this was day care, the year Gram and Grim took me over — and I had a thing about booting anyone who dared to touch me. Because they were *always* trying to throw a hug on me, like it was a medicine I needed.

Gram and Grim, bless their pointed little heads, they're my mother's people, *her* parents, and they figured whoa! better put this little critter with other little critters his own age, maybe it will improve his temper.

Yeah, right! Instead, what happened, I invented games like kick-boxing and kick-knees and kick-faces and kick-teachers, and kick-the-other-little-day-care-critters, because I knew what a rotten lie that hug stuff was. Oh, I *knew*.

That's when I got my first look at Freak, that year of the

phony hugs. He didn't look so different back then, we were all of us pretty small, right? But he wasn't in the playroom with us every day, just now and then he'd show up. Looking sort of fierce, is how I remember him. Except later it was Freak himself who taught me that remembering is a great invention of the mind, and if you try hard enough you can remember anything, whether it really happened or not.

So maybe he wasn't really all *that* fierce in day care, except I'm pretty sure he did hit a kid with his crutch once, whacked the little brat pretty good. And for some reason little Kicker never got around to kicking little Freak.

Maybe it was those crutches kept me from lashing out at him, man those crutches were cool. I wanted a pair for myself. And when little Freak showed up one day with these shiny braces strapped to his crooked legs, metal tubes right up to his hips, why those were even *more* cool than crutches.

"I'm Robot Man," little Freak would go, making these weird robot noises as he humped himself around the playground. *Rrrr . . . rrrr . . . rrrr . . .* like he had robot motors inside his legs, going *rrrrr . . . rrrr . . . rrrr*, and this look, like don't mess with me, man, maybe I got a laser cannon hidden inside these leg braces, smoke a hole right through you. No question, Freak was hooked on robots even back then, this little guy two feet tall, and already he knew what he wanted.

Then for a long time I never saw Freak anymore, one day he just never came back to day care, and the next thing I remember I'm like in the third grade or something and I catch a glimpse of this yellow-haired kid scowling at me from one of those cripple vans. Man, they were death-ray eyes, and I think, hey, that's him, the robot boy, and it was like whoa! because I'd forgotten all about him, day care was a blank place in my head, and nobody had called me Kicker for a long time.

Mad Max they were calling me, or Max Factor, or this one butthead in L.D. class called me Maxi Pad, until I persuaded him otherwise. Gram and Grim always called me Maxwell, though, which is supposed to be my real name, and sometimes I hated that worst of all. Maxwell, ugh.

Grim out in the kitchen one night, after supper whispering to Gram had she noticed how much Maxwell was getting to look like *Him*? Which is the way he always talked about my father, who had married his dear departed daughter and produced, eek eek, Maxwell. Grim never says my father's name, just *Him*, like his name is too scary to say.

It's more than just the way Maxwell resembles him, Grim says that night in the kitchen, the boy is *like* him, we'd better watch out, you never know what he might do while we're sleeping. Like his father did. And Gram right away shushes him and says don't ever say that, because little pictures have big ears, which makes me run to the mirror to see if it is my big ears made me look like *Him*.

What a butthead, huh?

Well, I *was* a butthead, because like I said, I never had a brain until Freak moved down the street. The summer before eighth grade, right? That's the summer I grew so fast that Grim said we'd best let the boy go barefoot, he's exploding out of his shoes. That barefoot summer when I fell down a lot, and the weirdo robot boy with his white-yellow hair and his weird fierce eyes moved into the duplex down the block with his beautiful brown-haired mom, the Fair Gwen of Air.

Only a falling-down goon would think that was her real name, right?

Like I said.

Are you paying attention here? Because you don't even know yet how we got to be Freak the Mighty. Which was pretty cool, even if I do say so myself.